Watch for other titles from

Cut Above Books

and

Noah Baird

at

www.secondwindpublishing.com

DONATIONS TO CLARITY

By

Noah Baird

Cut Above Books
Published by Second Wind Publishing, LLC.
Kernersville

Cut Above Books
Second Wind Publishing, LLC
931-B South Main Street, Box 145
Kernersville, NC 27284

First Cut Above Books edition published June 2011.
Cut Above Books, , Running Angel, and all production design are trademarks of Second Wind Publishing, used under license.

For information regarding bulk purchases of this book, digital purchase and special discounts, please contact the publisher at www.secondwindpublishing.com

Cover design by Santiago Uceda

Manufactured in the United States of America

ISBN 978-1-935171-44-7

To my father,
Thanks for not killing me when I was a teenager.

To my two favorite headaches,
I love you more than anything, but you really should stop shooting darts at me when I'm sleeping.

"Dear Sir or Madam, will you read my book?
It took me years to write, will you take a look?
It's based on a novel by a man named Lear
And I need a job, so I want to be a paperback writer."
             - Paul McCartney, Paperback Writer, 1966.

"I like a good story well told. That is the reason I am
sometimes forced to tell them myself."
             - Mark Twain, "The Watermelon" speech, 1907.

"If he was from Venus, would he feed us with a spoon?
If he was from Mars, wouldn't that be cool?
Standing right on campus, would he stamp us in a file?
Hangin' down in Memphis all the while."
             - Paul Westerberg, Alex Chilton, 1987.

1

"Beat on the Brat"

~Ramones

It takes 73 newtons of force to fracture a human skull. Roughly. Variations in bone thickness, age, and location of the blow introduce countless variables. A major league baseball player can lay wood on leather with 200 pounds of pressure or 890 newtons.

The skull was hit with 253 pounds of pressure or 1125 newtons. The blow was delivered with 20 percent more force than what a professional athlete would deliver. Over fifteen times the required force needed to crack an adult male's melon open. The entire swing took less than half a second. A 26-inch carbon steel baton weighing 1.46 pounds was used. Contact between baton and target lasted a precious 0.02 seconds. Faster than the 0.33 seconds required to blink, or the 0.878 seconds it took the victim's heart to pump one last time.

Ian King would have found this statistical information interesting. A welcome distraction from the butterflies surfing his own synapses. Ian even may have engaged the provider of such delicate morsels of information in conversation had it not been his skull used to provide the empirical data.

Green buds were sprouting on the tips of every branch in the forest. Mother Nature letting her hair down after the long winter. The season when children were lined up for crew cuts to prepare for warmer weather while Momma Nature was silently shaking her mane out. In three days, the buds would have opened and Ian would never have seen the footprint.

Two minutes before his last thought, Ian relaxed his pace. The sky had been full with rain and was now starting to drizzle. With the rain, the wind began to shift erratically. Ian stopped and adjusted his backpack and cracked his neck. He knew the pack would have difficulty picking up his scent with the wind shifting. He also knew the rain would mask the snapping twigs of his approach. He still needed to be careful. Eastern timber wolves were notoriously shy of humans.

Ian's thoughts drifted. The weather was warming, and warmth brought undergrads in shorts. He wondered what this year's batch would look like. He was in his third year of graduate work at the College of Environmental Science and Forestry. The curriculum required him to take undergrads out for fieldwork. The work could be gratifying unless he had to remind the students to take their earbuds out or stop texting. At least there were the girls.

Ian noted the pack's pace was focused over the last two days. Gone were the typical meanderings and backtracking. The wolves were moving quickly now, seldom stopping to rest. Ian knew he was anthropomorphizing, but he had a gut feeling the wolves knew they were in dangerous territory. What could be making the pack skittish? Ian rechecked the topography map and verified they were at least a half day's hike to the nearest civilization. It couldn't be humans making them pick up the pace.

Rain dropping on his face renewed his focus and he kneeled over with his tracking stick to pick up the stride of the pack lead. He glanced to his right and saw a familiar indentation in the mud. Nothing in nature resembles a human's silhouette. The same can be said for a human footprint. This particular print was nearly 18 inches long and deeply depressed into the mud. Ian jerked up with the realization of what he was looking at. He just connected the dots of why the wolves were quickly moving through the area when the baton struck his head.

A man dressed completely in black efficiently wiped the baton before collapsing it. He turned to an identically dressed man, "That ape is getting sloppy. Make contact with him and remind him of our position."

2

"Skating Away on the Thin Ice of a New Day"
~Jethro Tull

The delegation slowly began arriving and taking their usual place in the circle. One would think that, with some of the pedigrees in attendance, that this would be a moment of almost biblical proportions. One might think the attendees would crawl forth from the primordial ooze, arrive with a clap of thunder and a scent of sulfur, or descend from glowing balls in the sky, leaving only mysterious soot-calligraphy on some poor farmer's wheat field as the only evidence of their presence. One would not be wrong to think that— members of the delegation are legendary. Still they simply walked into the field and began slowly taking their place in the circle.

Standing in the center of the grouping were three men. They were dressed in identical black suits, and despite the hour, were wearing sunglasses. The suits, like the sunglasses, were neither hip nor classic. The suits fit well, but did not have a tailored look. These were not the suits of government public servants, nor were they the suits of the fashion savvy. Think of morticians, both sanitized and forgettable.

The human body is subject to three different forms of mortis shortly after it expires. Hollywood, either through half-assed research, or the desire to cram a loosely plausible plot into approximately forty-five minutes of digestible entertainment, has made rigor mortis, the stiffening of the limbs, the most familiar. The human vessel also undergoes algor mortis, the cooling of the body, as well as liver mortis, the pooling of blood caused by gravity pulling the blood toward the ground. The three men look like they have been visited by all three. Their bodies seem to be floating between expiration and the invitations going out announcing the decomposition party.

The tallest of the agents was very tall. His limbs seemed too long for his body, and each of his thin fingers seemed to have an additional phalange, casting the impression of a dead octopus hanging from each of his shirt cuffs. His sharp, asymmetrical face contorted into a permanent sneer, and he affected a sinister vibe of impatience, which kept even the silliest members of the delegation quiet. Temporarily, at least.

The Greys stake their territory on the northern edge of the group of delegates. Their choice of territory has less to do with cardinal heading, and more to do with the fact the ground slopes slightly higher on the northern portion of the field. They wax poetically of their desire to be closer to their home, the final frontier: space. It's really because they are really short and self-conscious about their height.

During last year's council meeting, all the Greys arrived wearing ten-inch '70s KISS boots, complete with demon faces and silver glitter. The rest of the delegation laughed so hard it took the Dark Agents thirty minutes to restore order. The snickering never quite stopped and not many issues were addressed.

The Greys were quieter this year. Ever since *X-Files* abdicated to reality television, the Greys had lost their collective spunkiness. They held onto their grandeur for as long they could, but once their

5

meticulously sculpted image had been twisted and mass marketed as little green aliens dressed as gangsta-rappers screenprinted onto boxer shorts, their collective spunk was blown. The P.L.A.N. had not worked for them.

The P.L.A.N. or Planned Liberation Assistance Network was a program created by the government to introduce or "naturalize", the term the Dark Agents preferred to use, those entities that lived beyond the edge of the human world. The delegation was made up of representatives from each race or community of entities whom the government wished to bring out of the shadows. The delegation met once a year to review the past year's progress, as well as to introduce the goals for the upcoming year.

Initially, the Sasquatch and Loch Ness representatives argued against the notion of naturalization of their kind. The fulcrum of their argument was their species has lived on the Earth long before humans came along. The Sasquatch cried species-ism while the Loch Ness Monsters remarked they should have eaten the humans when they had the chance.

The Dark Agents were eventually able to press the Sasquatch and Loch Ness representatives into complying with the P.L.A.N.

Eager for naturalization, the Moth Men already assembled a legal team ready to file a lawsuit against the United States government for discrimination on behalf of female Moth Men. Some of the Moth Men wanted a non-gender-specific name, and others suggested going a step further and dropping the "Moth" part of their name so not to be offensive to other living things. Some female Moth Men wanted to be referred to as "Moth Mothers," while others argued "Moth

Mothers" sounded too much like a stutter and could offend someone suffering with the affliction. Definitely something they would want to avoid if they ever hoped to become fully integrated with human society. Some trans/cross gender Moth Men wanted to be referred to as "Butterfly Balls."

No one could understand what the Chupracabre, the legendary Puerto Rican goat suckers, were saying, so no one knew if they wanted to live with the humans or not.

3

"Touch Me, I'm Sick"
~Mudhoney

"How much do you think the average human turd weighs?" Earl asked as he sat down at the table, pulling the plastic lawn chair up behind him and reaching across the table to dig into Harry's basket of buffalo wings.

"Are you serious? Why?" asked Harry.

"Well, answer me this: how much does an order of wings weigh?"

"Regular or jumbo?"

"Jumbo" Earl mumbled with a mouth full of meat, spraying Three Mile Island sauce across the table. Droplets of orange-tinged spit peppered the table. Earl snatched a paper towel off the roll sitting on the table and wiped the table once, leaving an arc of smeared wing sauce across the table.

"Dude! Say it, don't spray it!" Harry yelped, holding his beer out of the mist with one hand, while trying to cover a baskets of wings and celery sticks with the other hand.

"You know: my usual. How much do you think that weighs? The parts I eat?" Earl asked, craning his neck around looking for a waitress. Harry could hear the frustration in Earl's voice. Earl hadn't sat down with a beer, and he didn't usually like going for very long without one. Especially in The Beaver, not because the wings were too hot, but because Earl swore Yuengling tasted better from The Beaver's taps.

Everyone else in the village thought The Brown Beaver's draft beers tasted skunky because the staff never cleaned the lines. "That's bullshit!" Earl would bellow to anyone who would listen. Earl had the proud distinction of having been in two fistfights and arrested once for defending The Brown Beaver's honor. The second fight (and arrest) was with The Brown Beaver's owner, Seamus, who refused to give Earl any more alcohol one night.

"I don't know. Why?" Harry asked, responding to the back of Earl's head.

"I'm just trying to figure out how much I'm eating, is all," Earl said, holding up one finger to the waitress.

"What? Can't shop in the Miss's section anymore, Meatball?"

"Screw you! I'm serious!"

"Okay, okay. I'm sorry. Good for you! I'll support you on your diet. I hear they can be tough." Harry was switching gears, downshifting into sincerity drive, and hoping he sounded convincing or at least supportive.

"I'm not going a diet! I'm trying to figure out, in pounds, how much food I eat."

"Here you go, Earl" interrupted Cindi, placing his beer on the table.

"Well, thanks, darlin', and keep 'em coming." Earl cooed after taking a long drink. He gave Cindi his biggest smile, like a proud little boy showing his mama he ate all of his dinner.

"I sure will, honey." Cindi cooed back. She was a good waitress. She played along with the customers' little games, and ignored the slurred speech and rude pick up lines. She had wide hips and full breasts, her body was often described as good breeding stock by the old ranchers and lumberjacks sitting at the bar without their wives. She usually wore T-shirts with a low v-cut neckline when the weather was warm because she got better tips when she did.

"Cindi, how much does a jumbo order of wings weigh, not including the bones?" Earl probed, trying to sound intelligent in front of Cindi while still pumping out the charm.

"Uh, I don't know," Cindi responded sheepishly. *Why do customers always think of strange things to ask me?*

"No idea? Can you ask the cook how much an order of wings weighs without the bone? Do they weigh differently depending on the sauce?"

"Uh, sure," was all she could reply as she backed away from the table. *Why can't Earl do like Harry does and just stare at my tits instead of asking weirdo questions?*

"What's this have to do with turds?" Harry asked, watching Cindi's ass walk away.

"I'm trying to achieve neutral buoyancy within a human vessel." Earl deadpanned, also watching Cindi's ass walk away.

"Huh?"

"I said I was 'trying to achieve neutral buoyancy within a human vessel,' that is, me." Earl repeated with what he thought should be the impatient air of an academic.

"You see, Harry," Earl continued after taking a long pull from his beer, "I don't like taking shits." Earl stated, pausing for effect. Harry raised his eyebrows. Earl mistook the raised eyebrows as a signal to continue. "I'm tired of taking shits. It is the most despicable of all bodily functions," Earl continued, gaining speed. "Either through design or evolution, our waste disposal system is lacking. Our scatological process needs to be revamped. It's disgusting. It smells. It can be embarrassing. Leaves you feeling uncomfortable. I'm tired of it. I've done some research, and the average adult turd weighs between half of a pound to about a pound and a half."

"Really? That's it? I've had some whoppers I thought must've been heavier than that," replied Harry, his curiosity peaked, wrinkling his brow as he pondered Earl's latest bit of trivia. Another part of Harry's brain was simultaneously wondering why he was entertaining this conversation.

"I know. I thought the exact same thing," replied Earl, pleased Harry was showing some interest. "Anyway, I figure the weight of turds must equal the weight of excess food we consume. Food our body doesn't need." Earl was now punctuating the air with the fat end of a buffalo wing as he spoke. "So, I figure, if I reduce the amount of food I eat by the weight of my bowel movements, my body won't need to crap anymore. I will consume exactly what my body needs. So no waste. No more taking the Browns to the Super Bowl, or dropping the kids off at the pool! Close and seal the hatch. My crapping days are over."

Harry sat in amazement by the range of subjects Earl could pull out of his ass and discuss, without fear or embarrassment, in a public place. *Maybe sealing the hatch would be best?* "So, how's it going so far?" asked Harry, unconvinced.

"I'm still working on the ratio."

4

"Freak Magnet"
~Violent Femmes

Echo Clyne sat in front of her guest. The set of her news show was designed to look like a coffee shop. It was supposed to look cozier to the viewer than the sets of typical talk shows. The upholstery on one of the guest chairs was eggplant with random swirls and khaki blocks, the other guest chair was the exact opposite, khaki with eggplant blocks. The host's chair was a contemporary patchwork design with some of the patches looking like scraps from the warehouse where pimps' suits are made; squares of faux leopard and tiger fur. While other squares looked like the designer had gone on a hunting expedition in Dr. Seuss's universe. The coffee table was blond wood, and always had coffee mugs on it emblazoned with the news station's logo–a number nine centered in the pupil of an eye. The news station had hired a consulting company who'd designed the set. The highly paid consultants promised the set would seem like an extension of the viewer's living room, provided their living room was bought at Starbucks.

The set and the news anchor were part of a new segment introduced to bring the news station into the twenty-first century. More appetizing to today's discerning viewers, which meant the news station no longer covered the news. Today's discerning viewers were more interested in an endless stream of fluff pieces and celebrity incarcerations.

The news station also hired a PR team from the city to carefully construct a news segment based on extensive marketing research and analysis. The PR team created a new identity for the station which appeared to be relaxed, and not carefully constructed based on extensive marketing research and analysis. The general manager, Mangrove Slimebucket, would walk onto the set and interject nonsensical slogans to illustrate the vibe he was paying for. "I want more Walter Cronkite on tofu!" he would yell to the producer, as if the former Most Trusted Man in America would seem different if given a steady diet of soybean byproduct. Other helpful tidbits of advice included: "Give me Britney Spears wiping her ass with the Wall Street Journal!" and "Put Peter Jennings, a ground hog, and a frozen banana in a blender; that's what I want to see from a newscast!"

Echo was not happy to be interviewing Milo Backwater for this evening's segment. She stole a glance at Milo as a sound tech adjusted the placement of Milo's microphone. He was wearing a heavy chamois shirt, which always reminded Echo of washing her car, denim pants and work boots. For the interview, someone had brushed Milo's hair back and sealed it into place with some sort of shiny substance. Milo was also clean-shaven, and Echo could see the telltale cuts of razor nicks on his Adam's apple. Echo, nor anyone else, could remember Milo cleaned up. She looked him up and down, trying to decide if Milo had cleaned himself up, or if the station had sent someone to groom him. Echo imagined a team of butch beauticians, Queer Eye for the Straight Guy on steroids, infiltrating Milo's ranch with Batman belts of hygiene products, and a license to groom.

The last time Milo had performed this much

personal maintenance was his junior prom. Milo had even trimmed his toenails, and unknown to Echo, he was wiggling his little piggies in the now more spacious toe box of his work boots. The girl Milo was supposed to take to the prom, Mary Sloadvik, decided to trade up for another boy: Marty Paine, wide receiver for their high school football team, the Woodchucks. Crushed by the rejection, Milo gave up on most women and personal hygiene. Both were too complicated, he reasoned.

The technician finished adjusting Milo's microphone and walked off the set, leaving Echo and Milo alone. Echo, hyper-conscience of the fact they were going on the air in less than two minutes, tried to seem relaxed and friendly while simultaneously avoiding messing up her hair or her make-up; aware that every minute turn of her head moved her hair farther out of place.

Milo gazed around the studio, and generally looked uncomfortable. The set was harshly lit while the rest of the studio was dark. As if an enormous cookie-cutter was used to remove a coffee shop and drop it in the middle of a warehouse. It all reminded Milo of a deserted island centered in a dark sea. He thought he would be more comfortable with the technicians and production assistants than in front of the camera.

A young man with a ponytail and cargo pants walked up to the stage and announced, "We're on in 5, 4"; finishing the countdown silently by serially lowering three fingers as he backed away from the stage.

Echo launched into her intro, speaking directly to one camera, then another. Milo listened closely to Echo's intro, unconsciously nodding his head as she spoke. He was not sure if he was being filmed yet, or if the camera facing Echo was focused only on her. He discretely glanced around to see if a monitor was facing back at him, showing him the camera's view, like at the electronics section of Wal-Mart.

Echo's voice turned serious as she twisted in her chair to introduce Milo. "Milo Backwater, you recently had an extraordinary experience. Can you tell us about it?"

"Um, that's right, Echo. I was abducted," Milo stated nervously, quickly becoming aware of how difficult it was to speak in front of a camera.

Echo probed further, "Now when you say you were 'abducted,' you mean by beings from another planet?"

"Yes, ma'am. I was abducted by these little gray men. A lot of people think them aliens are green, but they're really grey like cement. They come into my house and took me on their spaceship."

"Milo, this must have been frightening for you. How did you know it was their spaceship? Were you able to see the Earth below you?"

"No, ma'am, I didn't see nothing like that. I was in a dark room, strapped to an examining table."

"'An examining table' onboard their spaceship," Echo clarified. "Were there windows in the room where you were held?"

"No, ma'am, just the table. It was like a doctor's office, but without the magazines, and the pictures, and the pamphlets on different diseases you could have, and the bottle of hand sanitizer on the wall. I don't think there was paper on the space examining table either," Milo added helpfully.

"Milo, can you recall how you were abducted? How did they get you into the spaceship?" Echo asked. She was determined to be professional about this interview. She wanted to interview Jezebel

Saddletramp, lead singer of the all-girl shock-rock group, The Fuck-Me-Pumps, on Jezebel's recent campaign to empower young girls by distributing self-help guides on how to become a dominatrix. The news station shot the idea down, and the interview with Milo Backwater was scheduled instead.

"Well, I don't know, to tell you the truth. I fell asleep watching TV and next thing I know, I wake up strapped to an examining table."

"And you don't remember being abducted?" Echo inquired.

"No, but I remember being probed." Milo deadpanned.

Echo attempted to clarify for the viewers, "Do you mean they conducted medical experiments on you?"

"No, I was probed," Milo stated.

"How were you probed?"

"I was probed in my orvis."

Momentarily losing her journalistic composure and forgetting about her make-up, Echo knitted her eyebrows together and bit her lower lip. All she could think of was fly fishing catalogs an ex-boyfriend used to get. Echo could hear the Doppler effect of her career traveling farther, and farther away. "You mean they examined your ears, nose . . ."

"They probed my orvis," Milo interrupted, catching himself before making a clarifying hand gesture on live television. "I didn't have a movement for a week."

Inside a spaceship in geostationary orbit above the Catskills, a crowd of cement colored aliens sat in front of a flat-screen TV laughing, while two Grays in the back of the room gave each other high-fives.

5

"Walking on Hell's Roof Looking at the Flowers"
~The Waco Brothers

He absentmindedly probed a raspberry seed stuck between two molars with his tongue as he walked; he seemed to always get a seed stuck between the same two teeth. He sniffed the air; deep, searching sniffs. The wind shifted and he picked up the scent again. Campfire smoke with subtle notes of silicon impregnated nylon, rip-stop canvas, and polyethylene water bottles. Campers.

He moved closer to the scents, taking an oblique route toward the river. He climbed part of the way up the side of the ridge, high enough to see above the low hawthorns and maple saplings, but below the main canopy of the forest. From this vantage, he could see further through the forest while giving himself an escape route. With his long strides; he knew he could climb the ridge faster than any human. Soon he could tell by the scent of the campfire that he was at the closest point along his route to the campers, and he crept down the ridge toward the scent. He could hear noises now as well. Muffled at first, punctuated by girlish laughter, but now clearer. He could make out four voices: two male, two female.

For all his size and bulk, he could move quietly through the woods. Conscience of his scent, he moved downwind from the campsite and crept closer to the campers until he could see the flicker of the campfire dancing on the tree trunks ahead of him. He peered between the two trunks of an oak that had divided about six feet up from the forest floor. He could see the campers, paired up into couples, sitting around a fire. Two dome shaped tents were arranged several feet apart with the main entrances opening towards the campfire area. From this vantage point, he could see inside both tents. Four kayaks were laid together up from the bank of the river, each with a paddle and gear stacked nearby.

The couples sat on self-inflating, accordion chairs; the kind where the chair cushions are removed and used as the pad under a sleeping bag. One woman, the blond, took off sandals that looked like the result of some sort of gladiator/amphibian crossbreeding, and stretched her legs towards the fire.

He sized the couples up and judged by the organic cotton clothing and fashionable outdoor gear that these weren't hunters, and probably weren't armed. He peered into the woods past the campsite and saw it. Twelve feet off the ground dangled the food container tied to a limb of a sugar maple. The food container was a bear resistant type, made of high-impact plastic. The containers were supposed to be difficult for bears to get into, but are hung from trees to keep the food out of the bruins' reach, just in case.

There has not been a reported case of a factory warranty stopping a bear from eating the food.

The factory warranty for the bear resistant food container did not have a disclaimer regarding Bigfoot.

Interview with Echo Clyne:

Lindsey (Camper): "I was purifying my water

when I smelled this stench. I have this UV light-pen to kill any bacteria in the water, but then I wondered if the UV light works as well because the river water has a bunch of tannic acid in it. So the river looks like tea, you know? Maybe the UV light can't get to all of the bacteria. Anyway, so first I use my UV light-pen to kill all the bacteria it can, then I pour the water into a three-stage water purification system. The first stage is an adjustable ceramic pre-filter to eliminate the suspended particles up to 0.2 microns; the second stage is a glass fiber filter which filters out any bacteria down to 0.1 microns. The third stage is an active charcoal filter to eliminate all of the odors. Then I hit the water again with the UV pen just to make sure there's nothing else swimming in there. Finally, I run the water through a mixed oxidant purifier, which makes your water into brine and then passes an electrical charge to eliminate any bacteria, viruses, and protozoa. I pour the water into one of my BPA-free aircraft grade aluminum water bottles from Switzerland. Then I usually mix a powdered juice packet in it because I really don't like the taste of water.

Anyway. I smell this stench. I don't know what it was, but it smelled like something was dead. Not even Dylan can smell that bad. Then I thought someone didn't dig a hole to bury their crap. I've told them not to relieve themselves within two hundred feet of the river, and everything has to go into a hole at least 6 inches deep. I brought a shovel with an integrated flashlight and depth gauge just for that purpose."

Dylan (Camper): "My mother used to say: 'The hen that squawks first laid the egg.' Lindsey is always complaining about smells. I couldn't believe it. We've been camping and kayaking for four days. Of course there's a stench."

Cynthia (Camper): "Okay, I did have stinky gas, but that wasn't me. I couldn't help it. It's all that freeze-dried food Dylan and Lindsey brought. Plus, I'm surfing the crimson tide. I get all bloated and gassy, but that stench didn't come out of me. Whatever."

Ross (Camper): "I didn't smell anything. The campfire smoke was bothering my allergies and my sinuses were all clogged up.
I did see the rock land in the middle of the campsite."

Dylan (Camper): "I'm 27 years old. Jim Morrison, Jimi Hendrix, Janice Joplin, and Kurt Cobain all died at 27. I knew I couldn't die yet. I haven't made something beautiful. I have three months, one week, and five days to create my *Are You Experienced* or my *Nevermind*. That rock really scared the shit out of me. How long do you think it would take to learn to play the guitar?"

Cynthia (Camper): "Okay. How surreal was that? We're talking, hanging out, you know, and this huge rock comes flying through the woods and lands right in the middle of the campsite. The rock nearly landed in the fire. I peed myself; just a little, maybe about a tablespoon. What's weird is: all I could think in that moment was suggesting we all go swimming so no one would know I squirted myself. You aren't going to print this are you?"

Lindsey (Camper): "I have this super bright

flashlight, called a 'Cat Fire.' It comes standard with a 65 lumens bulb, but I scored a military grade 120 lumens bulb off the internet. At 120 lumens, this flashlight is used by police and paramilitary forces as a non-lethal deterrent. It's so bright it will stun you. I don't use it all of the time because it sucks batteries dry. I use a halogen headlamp for cruising around the woods, and I have a solar powered light that attaches to a water bottle. It's awesome. The water in the bottle refracts the light to create a rechargeable lantern, which I use around the campsite."

Ross (Camper): "The place we were camping, our campsite, was in a flat area. That rock didn't roll down a hill. There's a ridge that intersects with the river, but it was a quarter mile away from where we were. It didn't roll into our camp. We would've heard it roll. Someone or something threw that rock. But the thing is: I don't know anyone who could've thrown a rock like that. The rock was bigger than a basketball. Let me rephrase that: I know people who can throw a rock that size. I could throw a rock that size a couple of feet. I don't know anyone who could have thrown a rock that size from far enough away that we couldn't see them with the light from the campfire. We could easily see thirty, maybe forty feet in every direction."

Dylan (Camper): "Dude, I definitely couldn't have thrown that boulder that far. Somebody launched that thing. The boulder didn't bounce or roll when it landed. It landed so hard it left a crater at least seven inches deep. The whole ground shook."

Cynthia (Camper): "Oh-my-gosh, I let out this scream, it could've shattered glass. Dylan let out this noise like he was saying 'hey' and 'yeah' at the same time while riding down a bumpy road. Not a girly scream but a shaken scream. It seems funny to think of that now. Weird, huh? Anyway, the rock makes this crazy loud sound when it lands, like 'boom'! That's what made me squirt a little."

Lindsey (Camper): "So I whip out the Cat Fire, and shine it around the campfire. This flashlight is amazing. It's like holding a magic wand, and casting daylight wherever I point the beam. It's weird, too. The beam creates a bunch of shadows from all of the branches and leaves. As I move the beam of light it seems the entire forest is moving and twisting with the beam. It was hard to focus on anything moving because of all the shadows shifting around.

I swung the light towards where we had our food container. That's when we heard the roar. I can only describe it: you know those dinosaur movies where the t-rex roars? It was like that but way, way, way louder, and it was in the fucking woods with us."

Dylan (Camper): "I don't know how I didn't piss myself. It was easily the loudest sound I've ever heard. I didn't just hear the roar; I felt it. It rattled my bones. I always thought that was an expression people used."

Ross (Camper): "It was like a wave of sound. It's like when someone pours a cup of ice-cold water on you when you are in the shower.

I don't know who started running first, but we just all seemed to start running in different directions. I heard Lindsey yell to go to the kayaks. I don't know why that sounded like such a good idea at the time. The river isn't very deep here. I guess we were lost in the fight or flight response. Trading domains just sounded like a good idea; it was on land so we should be on the water."

Lindsey (camper): "I just ran for the kayaks. The whole forest seemed to explode. I could hear the sound of running footsteps and bodies crashing through vegetation in every direction. I just ran for the kayaks. I didn't know everyone else followed me until we rallied down river."

Dylan (Camper): "We tied the kayaks together in the middle of the river, and I held onto a branch sticking out of the water from a submerged tree to keep from drifting. None of us brought our flashlights in the panic. I figured we'd be able to hear the thing splashing in the water if it decided to come for us."

Cynthia (Camper): "The woods are freaky at night if you don't have any light. It's totally dark and sounds seem to carry forever. It's like the woods breathe in light and exhale sound."

Lindsey (camper): "I actually had my Cat Fire with me. It was on a lanyard around my wrist, but I wasn't going to turn it on. I wasn't going to piss that thing off again."

Ross (Camper): "We could hear something going through our tents and gear. Our campfire was still burning, and we could see something moving around the camp. It was hard to tell the size; mostly I saw its shadow moving around. The shadow looked huge, but I didn't have a point of reference to compare it to."

Dylan (Camper): "I can't be sure, but it looked like whatever it was walked down to the river's edge to watch us. It was hard to tell, but it looked like it walked like a person, and it seemed to be pulling out something held in its arms and pouring something in its mouth. When we went back to shore the next morning; every package of instant oatmeal we had was torn open and the empty wrappers were left on the riverbank. Right where that thing had been standing. The only flavor of oatmeal packets not eaten were the banana nut flavor Lindsey brought. Only one of those was ripped open, and it looked like the contents were spit out."

Cynthia (Camper): "It was that fake banana flavor. I hate that flavor too."

Lindsey (camper): "Hey! I like that oatmeal."

Supplemental interview with Bigfoot: *Fake banana flavor bad. Why can't make descent banana flavor? Humans manufacture every other flavor, but no can make banana flavor. I know can't use real banana. Bigfoot love peanut butter banana sandwich. Know why no banana jelly? Banana brown when cooked. Look like shit. Bigfoot no eat. Bigfoot no like fake banana flavor. Bigfoot only like sandwich with real banana. It hard for Bigfoot to find banana in woods. Banana no grow here. Bigfoot need scare lot of camper to find camper with banana. Most camper carry apple. Bigfoot so tired of apple. Apple grow everywhere here. Peanut butter and apple sandwich good too, but not as good as banana.*

Ross (Camper): "It ate nearly everything; enough food to feed four adults for three days. That's breakfast, lunch, and dinner, plus snacks. It even ate the emergency three day supply of military surplus MREs (Meals Ready to Eat) I keep in my gear. Those things are 1200 calories each; 3600 calories per day. That thing ate three days of meals; over 10,000 calories. Under normal circumstances, an average person consumes 2000 calories a day. It ate five days worth of calories, plus all of our food we had tied up in the tree. It should've popped like a balloon. If anybody was interested, you could probably start looking for it now. You'll know you're near it if you find a bowel movement the size of a water cooler jug.

The strange thing is it didn't look like an animal got into the food. The wrappers weren't chewed in to, and the contents weren't spilled everywhere, like what an animal would do. The wrappers were opened like a human did it. The MRE chemical heater packs look like they had been used correctly. The bear-proof container hadn't been gnawed or scratched. If you've ever seen what a bear will do to groceries; they destroy everything they touch. This wasn't anything like that. It was like a human raided our camp, but from what we saw and heard. It wasn't human."

Supplemental interview with Bigfoot: *These campers no have nice selection for Bigfoot. Too much vegetable and no meat. Only vegetable, rice, noodle. Why eat so healthy? Need peanut butter and chocolate. Also shitty trail mix. Only buy trail mix with dried fruit and seeds. I give to raccoons. They eat anything. Need to buy trail mix with chocolate candy and peanuts. That Bigfoot like.*

Also, no whiskey or cigarette. Only hunter carry whiskey and cigarette. Bigfoot like. Hard for Bigfoot use lighter. Need scare hunter when first light cigarette. Hope not menthol.

Teenager have funny cigarette and beer. Beer nice but make Bigfoot fat. One teenager have pills. Make Bigfoot want mate everyone. Bigfoot find She-Bigfoot. She follow Bigfoot around for month after that. Bigfoot try run and hide. Now she and other She-Bigfoots talk bad about Bigfoot. Say Bigfoot smell. Say Bigfoot only want visit her when Bigfoot drink whiskey. She-Bigfoot want be couple in morning. Bigfoot no want. Then she want talk closure. Bigfoot know what closure mean. She-Bigfoot think closure mean she talk all bad things Bigfoot do: Bigfoot lazy, Bigfoot stink, Bigfoot drink too much, Bigfoot no get flower, Bigfoot hang out with circus freaks too much. That not what closure mean.

She say Bigfoot asshole when Bigfoot drink whiskey. Bigfoot say she bitch when Bigfoot drink whiskey. Maybe Bigfoot no drink whiskey. Whiskey make She-Bigfoot want to tell Bigfoot all his bad habit. Bigfoot not know Bigfoot have so many bad habit.

Want She-Bigfoot to drink whiskey. Want whiskey make She-Bigfoot want mate and no talk. Whiskey maybe make She-Bigfoot want get Bigfoot food and no talk. Whiskey make She-Bigfoot talk more and want to tell Bigfoot all his problem. Bigfoot know why hunter drink alone in woods.

Cynthia (Camper): "It went through our tents too. It looked like it was holding something to its face and sniffing it from my tent. It kinda looked liked it was rubbing things on its cheek, like you do with something soft. We got back to camp, my favorite fleece jacket was gone. I loved that jacket."

Ross (Camper): "It took my glasses. I was wearing my contacts. I usually switch to glasses at night, but I hadn't that night. I was stuck wearing my contacts until I got home. I perforated my cornea by wearing my contacts so long."

Supplemental interview with Bigfoot: *Bigfoot have bad eyes! What? Human only think human have bad eyes? Bigfoot have bad eyes. Animals have bad eyes. There bear in woods with bad eyes and bad nose. Always think Bigfoot girl bear. Want to make cub with Bigfoot. Bear no wear eyeglasses Bigfoot give him. Say make bear look like nerd. Bigfoot have to run from horny bad eyesight bear.*

Lindsey (camper): "It took nearly everything I had. It took my self-inflating sleeping pad. My sleeping pad was being used as the cushion of my camp chair. Whatever it was deflated the pad, rolled it up, and put it in the compression sack. It took my sleeping bag. I don't know what it would want to do with it; it's a woman's sleeping bag. My tent. It took my tent! Let me paint a picture: my tent wasn't torn down or dragged around through the woods. Something didn't tear through the fly. Oh no, my tent was packed and removed from the area."

Dylan (Camper): "It took all of our gear: tents, sleeping bags, lanterns, soap, water bottles, stoves, packs; everything. It was like we were never there. It even took our shoes.
We still had our kayaks. There was nothing we could do but paddle down river to the nearest town. That's when we called the police. The police just laughed when we told them our story."

Supplemental interview with Bigfoot: *Bigfoot no*

understand human. Human think live in forest so nice. Human make clothes smell like shit. Think smell like woods. Human want clothes smell spring fresh, mountain dew, summer garden. Clothes no smell like outside. Human have paper pine tree in car. Bigfoot like paper tree color. Break into car. Paper pine tree smell like someone shit on pinecone. Human have bad sense of smell.

I see magazine picture where human put bed in forest; like that nice place to sleep. Human like to think they like sleep outside. Know what animal think about? Sleep in human house! That why human pets always want come inside. Sleep in forest hard. Bigfoot get rain on, snow on. Bugs bite Bigfoot. Bigfoot have flea problem; no make flea collar for Bigfoot. Horny bears always want sneak into Bigfoot den when Bigfoot sleep. Try spoon Bigfoot.

Human want sleep in forest but bring whole house to forest. Human want to sleep outside but not too uncomfortable. Bigfoot no have self-inflating mattress. Bigfoot make bed of leaves and moss. Bigfoot no have rake. It hard to rake leaves into pile for Bigfoot. Horny bear come at night say only want cuddle. Bigfoot have to look for new den, make new bed . . .

Ross (Camper): "I've been camping all of my life; I have a degree in physical anthropology. That was not a bear and it wasn't human. No human could make that sound. What do I think it was? Do you want me to say we were mugged by Bigfoot? I'm not ready to say what we saw. I can't get my head around the idea yet of what happened to us."

Cynthia (Camper): "I saw Bigfoot and I peed my pants."

6

"Passenger Side"

~Wilco

"We've got a new sighting!" Roy shouted, twisting his head to project his voice out of the room. "A solid Class Five incident with, get this, four Type A witnesses. All four witnesses are college educated, experienced campers. They were kayak-camping when the incident happened. One witness even worked two summers for a canoe expedition outfitter back in college. All four appear to have been sober and fairly well rested. The full story will be on WTFU Channel 9 at five o'clock and again at ten." Roy picked up his half-gallon mug of Diet Mountain Dew and sucked the neon liquid up through a sweaty accordion straw that looked like it has never been introduced to soap.

"Where?" A voice inquired from another room.

"New York."

"Upstate?"

"Nope. Manhattan," Roy said.

"Really? I thought all of the campers in Manhattan were called bums."

"I don't think that's very P.C. I think they are now referred to as 'Residentially Deprived.'"

"I stand corrected, sir." The voice and it's owner, Jeff, wandered into the room. Jeff was tall and lanky; wearing pressed khaki pants, topsiders, and a pale blue golf shirt. The shirt had a large embroidery on the left chest with a SRO (Sasquatch Research Organization) centered in the middle of a large footprint. Jeff's clean cut appearance was the exact opposite of his partner's. Roy was dressed in Mossy Oak camouflaged pants, jungle boots, and a T-shirt with the words "I Believe In Bigfoot-I dated his sister" screen-printed on it. They were yin and yang. Roy was *X-Files* geek to Jeff's FBI agent fashion.

"Search for any investigators in the area who could respond."

"Already working it," replied Roy, his fingers making clickety-click sounds on the keyboard while he sighed loudly to himself. "I don't think there is anyone. We're the closest. I did find a website of a company in the area offering tours of the local Bigfoot sightings. Actually, it's a pretty cool website; awesome graphics."

Jeff bent over Roy's shoulder to get a better look at the computer screen. "Southern Tier Bigfoot Tours, huh? They can't be legit. New York doesn't have enough Bigfoot sightings to support a tour company."

"True, but they've got to know the area. We can contact them to be guides," reasoned Roy.

"I don't like it, but I don't think we have choice. Click the contact link and I'll give them a call."

The website window updated to the contact page. "Here you go. It looks like its run by three guys: Earl, Harry, and someone named Patch."

7

"Born With a Tail"
~Woodbox Gang

Ted Carp had been different all his life. Not in the "You may feel different, just like everyone else" sort of way. Not even the "You're only as crazy as your thoughts" sort of way. Ted wasn't even different in the "Clockwork Orange, shave off your nipple, understanding Pink Floyd on a much deeper level" sort of way. Ted Carp was different in the "lost within himself" sort of way. Introspective to the point where Ted had no natural reactions. Ted pondered the butterfly effect of choosing asparagus over broccoli. Then he pondered the olfactory implications of his choice. What if he chose the asparagus, which he really wanted, and he met a women and she rejected him because his urine had a strong odor? Every action, feeling, and behavior was deciphered and analyzed until Ted could no longer function socially. According to the *DSM IV* (*Diagnostic and Statistical Manual of Mental Disorders*, Fourth Edition) and the highly educated psychiatrists trained to read it, Ted was schizophrenic with paranoid delusions. Ted just thought he liked to smoke cigarettes with Bigfoot.

Of course you can't just tell people you smoke with Bigfoot. You'll get more medicine if you tell people. Ted had told the therapist once. Not because he was so naïve to think anyone would believe him. He told the therapist because, as part of his treatment, the therapist had urged him to share and trust more. So Ted Carp looked the recently minted therapist directly in the eye and told her about his smoke breaks with Bigfoot. Just like he knew she would: she upped his meds.

Ted argued against the new medication on the grounds the prescription was boosted in response to him opening up during his trust therapy. To which the therapist pointed out Ted was also paranoid. Ted pointed out paranoia is an irrational fear. If he feared getting a higher prescription, which is exactly what happened, then he couldn't be paranoid because his fear had been proven to be rational. After lecturing Ted on being difficult and evasive; she upped his meds again.

Domino Chipolte was Ted's second therapist this year. He liked to think of his female therapists as girlfriends. Girlfriends who took playing hard to get to a new level, but the girlfriend label worked for Ted. They asked far too many questions, and they were evasive if a question was asked of them; just like a girlfriend. They always wanted to know what he was thinking, and they were never satisfied when he said that he wasn't thinking of anything; just like a girlfriend. They tended to be very opinionated, and never seemed to get tired of telling Ted all of the ways he could improve himself; just like a girlfriend. But they eventually did get tired, and they became frustrated with him. Then they left; just like a girlfriend. This too worked for Ted. Girlfriends also became tired of Ted, and frustrated when he wouldn't change. So they too came and went; like the ebb and flow of waves. Just like a surfer never mourns a passing wave, Ted never mourned a passing therapist/girlfriend. There was always another wave coming. The state had mandated it.

Ted was a "resident patient" of a state run mental hospital, and had been for two years. The state preferred the term "resident patient" to describe the recipients of the state-sponsored mental health care. Ted preferred "Court Mandated Prisoner." "Resident" seemed to imply a choice. Like Ted *chose* to live in a secure hospital with guards, and fences topped with barbed wire, and a twenty-four hour staff monitoring his daily activities. Ted reasoned "prisoner" was a more accurate description of his incarceration.

Not that living in a mental hospital was all bad. Initially, Ted had been nearly overcome by panic attacks when the judge delivered his sentence. Up to that point in Ted's life, he hadn't had any really serious interactions with the law. What little of prison Ted knew about came from cable television, which only made him wonder if he was going to be required to prove his Caucasian ancestry to the resident chapter of the Aryan Nation. How did you prove ancestry under those conditions? Apparently, according to the cable TV shows, he couldn't just walk in and state: "Look at me: I'm a honky, both my parents are honkies, their parents were honkies . . ."

Not that Ted was racist or particularly proud of his ancestry. Never one to put little Irish flag stickers on his car, or hang a flag from his review mirror; Ted regarded race like a cow regards the color of grass it's eating. His ancestry was a simple fact. He never experienced the tug and pulls of ancestral gravity causing a sea of emotion to rise and fall. He was never homesick for the home he's never had. He never daydreamed about going back to the old country to see where his family came from. Ted didn't know anyone over in Ireland nor did he care if they were related. He never knew those people and probably never would. Never claimed to be "Irish" or "Irish-American"; Ted hardly even viewed himself as simply "American." He never understood Americans who wore T-shirts with screen-printed slogans like "These Colors Don't Run" or "America: Love It or Leave It." It was too "preaching to the choir" for Ted. Wearing a "These Colors Don't Run" T-shirt in Georgia didn't do much. Wearing the same shirt while wandering the backstreets of Baghdad; that was patriotic.

Now Ted was going to have to join some prison Nazi party to keep from becoming somebody's sex slave. Ted envisioned he had no other choice. The whole idea made Ted nauseous.

It turned out in a mental hospital there were three types of skinheads, and Ted didn't need to worry about any of them. The first type was the pseudo-skinhead who shaved his head as more of a fashion statement than a political ideology; unless you considered trying to look like a badass an ideology. There had been a regrettable episode when Ted first arrived at the hospital where he pledged allegiance to one of these skinheads. The misunderstanding really turned out to be pretty embarrassing for both people involved. The second type of skinhead was the type of patient whose head was shaved involuntarily by the hospital staff because the patent lacked proper grooming habits. Ted had another embarrassing episode when he pledged allegiance to one of these skinheads, who immediately began screaming in Ted's face, which Ted took as some sort of initiation. The third type of skinhead was the type who simply tore the hair out of their heads. That type had more of a slapdash, one-sided, patchy skinhead look. Ted didn't bother pledging allegiance to anyone looking like that.

It also turned out there weren't any rapists in the hospital, at least none interested in Ted. In fact, living in a mental hospital was liberating for Ted. Free of the burdens of modern American societal ideals and desires. Nobody cared what coffee Ted drank, or car he drove, or how much money he made, or shoes he wore, or what TV shows he watched. In a mental hospital, Ted could be free of the facets we use to establish who we are. Hairstyles and running shoe were no longer demarcating choices which compartmentalized him into one category or another. The saying: "You are what you owe" simply couldn't be applied anymore. Ted also found he was liberated from the social norms used to define civilized behavior. He could burp, fart, scratch, scream, grunt and talk to himself without embarrassment or care.

He could sing. He sang all of his favorite songs-loudly, in front of anyone because nobody was in a position to judge. He made up dirty limericks about the other "residents" for his own amusement.

The experience reminded him of the week-long camping trips his father took him on with his uncles where civilized standards were left behind and were replaced by new primal behavior. However, the new behavior didn't seemed truly new, but more of a temporary reverse evolution in behavior. *Medulla oblongata* muscle memory from Neanderthal ancestry. Only in a mental hospital, he could push the behavior longer than a week. In fact, he could do whatever he wanted. Ted spent weeks speaking in what he imagined to be a posh British voice just to see what would happen; which was nothing. He invented new characters to act like to entertain himself and the other "residents." He pretended to be a homophobic firefighter from Boston on vacation and the hospital was a hotel on a tropic island. For a week he pretended to be a southern Civil War general inspecting a fort. Ted treated patients and staff alike as characters in his role-playing games. Sometimes he stayed in character for weeks. Sometimes he stayed in character so long he had trouble getting out of the character, and he'd struggle to remember who he was before he started pretending to be someone else.

Ted used the characters to cover his own self-discovery. For Ted, living in a mental hospital was a lot like getting out of a long-term relationship. He felt like a drogue chute had been removed and he was being flung forward. Now he could discover what he liked and disliked on his own, without having to absorb someone else's thoughts on the matter. He could have his own emotions and opinions about things without worrying how that will affect everyone else. He was free to figure out who Ted really was, and not who Ted pretended to be to everyone else. Only in a place where everyone had a loose grasp on reality could you honestly be free to be yourself.

The upside? You could have all the drugs you wanted.

He first met Bigfoot when he was smoking outside while walking along the hospital's perimeter fence. Ted didn't normally smoke. Ted hadn't smoked for years; not since college. In college he always smoked one Marlboro red after smoking a joint. Ted didn't really know why, but a college roommate, a self-proclaimed Grand Poobah of Bong Hits, claimed it helped balance out the high. The smoky addition became tradition after that stony declaration.

Now Ted was smoking as part of the character he was submerged in: a chain-smoking, whiskey-voiced barfly. Ted hadn't developed an occupation for the character yet. He'd wait to see where the barfly dialogue would take him. He even learned to talk with a lit cigarette in his mouth without shutting one eye;

Keith Richards style.

Ted had just lit up a cigarette when a large, fur-covered hand reached over the fence that surrounded the mental hospital grounds and began waiving Ted over. The brush on the outside of the fence was thick and there were several trees which created large shadows, making it difficult for Ted to see what the large, fur-covered hand was attached to. Ted strolled over to where the hand was now performing a rapid arm sweeping motion which looked like the international sign for *Get your ass over here*. Ted realized, as he was walking towards the hand, that he probably shouldn't be walking towards large, fur-covered hands that waved at you from the woods. He assumed this was one of the inadvertent side effects he developed while a "resident": after living in a mental hospital long enough, not much surprised you anymore.

The large, fur-covered hand was now gesticulating frantically towards the lit cigarette in Ted's hand. Then making the two-finger holding a cigarette gesture, and moving the hand up to the area Ted assumed to be the face. Although he still couldn't see anything other than the hand. Ted held out his cigarette for the hand when the hand stopped gesturing suddenly, and began waiving him off. Then the hand pointed to Ted's jacket pocket and resumed the holding a cigarette between two fingers motion again. Ted fished out a new cigarette from the pack and lit it while the large, fur-covered hand waived excitedly. It's long fingers performed the greedy *gimmie, gimmie, gimmie* motion children perfected long ago. The large, fur-covered hand quickly grabbed the lit cigarette and retreated over the fence to where Ted could no longer see it.

Ted stood there awkwardly waiting for something else to happen. The thought occurred to Ted that perhaps he was crazy, and he had not just given a lit cigarette to a large, fur-covered hand. Ted could hear the hand's owner sucking and exhaling, and he could see puffs of smoke rhythmically being blown out from the bushes. After a couple of minutes, the smoking cigarette butt was sent sailing across the fence and the large, fur-covered hand began gesturing for another cigarette. This happened four more times. For each cigarette, Ted stood awkwardly by the fence, like a stranger waiting to break into an intimate conversation. After the final cigarette butt went flying over the fence, the large, fur-covered hand reached across the fence and patted Ted on the head, and retracted back into the bushes. Ted could hear the hand–and presumably the rest of the body–moving through the bushes away from him, deeper into the woods.

Ted went to the same spot every day, and each time the large, fur-covered hand waived to him as he approached. Eventually, Ted saw more of the corporeal body the large, fur-covered hand was attached to. It was a massive creature covered in long brown hair. It was large–extremely large. It was easily the largest biped Ted had ever seen. Standing next to the creature was similar to standing next to a very large horse. It, he, looked not quite ape, not quite Neanderthal, not quite dog. His overall appearance seemed brutal, primitive. After seeing him, Ted knew where the stories of ogres, trolls, and giants must have come from. His eyes were intelligent, even gentle at times. Some of the hair on the shoulders, back, and chest looked to be tipped in black. The skin on the palms of the hand looked dark. His face was partially covered in brown fur and the exposed areas were covered in dark skin. The nose was flat with prominent nostrils. The eyes were dark brown and shadowed by a heavy brow covered in fur. The mouth area protruded some, not like a snout; more like a chimpanzee's. The mouth was full of yellow and brown teeth, like dog or bear teeth. Ted was tempted to bring a toothbrush and a tube of toothpaste on his daily smoke breaks. He wasn't hideous, but he could see how someone might think that. He also wasn't beautiful. This wasn't a show dog bred to the pinnacle of aesthetic perfection, nor was this the wild wolf photographed in nature magazines and calendars; picture perfect examples of wild beauty. Bigfoot's appearance was imperfection personified. His appearance was the difference between organic fruit compared to genetically engineered fruit. He vaguely resembled the photographs of adult chimpanzees, with the pink skin of youth lost to splotches and uneven pigmentation.

Ted knew exactly what he was as soon as he saw him. This was another side effect of living in a mental hospital: your mind could clutch at the most impossible, or at the very least, the most unlikely of conclusions without any unnecessary reflection. Bigfoot visits you everyday to smoke cigarettes? Sure! Why the fuck not? It was like being mugged for the first time. Everyone has heard the stories, read the articles, saw it in the news, but it all seems abstract until it's happening to you. Then it becomes surreal. Now there's a person made of flesh and blood, with a name, a social security number, who'd probably had the flu in the 8th grade, maybe even cried during *Free Willy*. Now this person, this former sensitive little boy is now a man and sticking a gun in your face demanding your wallet. The dichotomy of the situation fragments and polarizes your brain, and you step back to become the observer to your own life. You see you calmly reach into the right pocket of your pants and remove your wallet. You see you hand your wallet over to the man with a gun. You see you flinch and stumble to the ground after the man with the gun smacks you in the temple with the butt of the gun. You see you bleeding on the ground while your mind applies sights, sounds, and scents to your predicament. It's the smell that solidifies the memory. Smell knocks you back into reality; tells your brain what is happening is really what is happening. Smell always brings the brain back; grounds it in the *now*.

And Bigfoot stinks. He smelled like a mixture of body odor, musk, rotting food, and sex. The odor was strong enough to knock Ted back whenever Ted was caught downwind of him. How the hell these things have remained elusive with a stink like that, Ted could not understand. He wanted to tell someone, anyone, that the way to find Bigfoot was not by the footprints, but by the stink. There was no hiding from that.

"So what does Bigfoot mean to you?" Ted was sitting across from Domino Chipotle as she launched the beginning salvo of questions which always set the tone for the session. She was wearing khaki Capri pants, a pale blue linen blouse stitched with hippy-looking embroidery, and vegan Mary Janes. Her blond hair was pulled back into a sloppy ponytail, and she wore tortoiseshell-framed eyeglasses.

"What does Bigfoot mean to you?" she repeated.

Ted shifted in his seat and looked at Domino. She insisted he refer to her as Ms. Chipotle. Ted refused, claiming he'd be more comfortable if they were on a first name basis.

"Bigfoot doesn't mean anything to me. Well, I suppose he does now. I guess he's a companion, a friend from outside of here." Ted spread his arms out like he was giving a huge person a hug to demonstrate the "here."

"By 'here,' Ted, do you mean 'here' at the hospital or . . ."

"Yes, here, as in the asylum" Ted responded with the air of a patient boyfriend.

Ignoring Ted's politically incorrect terminology, Domino continued, "Why do you think you see things from the outside world as creatures which don't exist? Do you feel anxious about the world outside this hospital?"

Ted smiled and sighed at Domino. He really hoped this relationship worked out. She was really playing it professional, but Ted thought he sensed some cracks in her occupational armor. He could tell in her eyes. "No. I see him as a friend from outside the asylum because he lives on the other side of the fence. The side without the asylum."

Noticing the cigarette box shaped bulge in Ted's pocket, Domino shifted directions. "I didn't know you smoked Ted. I shouldn't need to tell you this, but those things are horrible for your health."

"I, uh, don't normally smoke, just occasionally" Ted lied. Embarrassed and self-conscious about cigarette odor, he imagined the ashtray breath would be a hurdle for their budding relationship. Well, there will be things they would learn about each other which they may not care for, but they will need to get past those if this relationship was going to work.

8

"Suspicious Minds"
~Elvis Presley

"GPS says this is the location. The terrain matches the witnesses' description," said Jeff, slowly turning in a circle while holding a small GPS unit in front of him. Jeff was dressed in khaki hiking pants; the kind with zippers on the legs so they can be converted into shorts. His dry-weave polo shirt was tucked in and his hiking boots were new. He carried a large nylon backpack. The over-all effect was vaguely Star Trek landing party chic. The GPS might as well have been a tricorder.

"Thank God! How far did we hike?" Roy panted as he exploded through the brush. All of his clothes were dark with sweat.

"Five point two miles."

"Hhmm. Seemed a lot longer." Roy was still panting heavily and wiping his face on his shirt. His belly hung obscenely over his pants. A white gelatinous mass frozen mid-pour. A non-Newtonian fluid, neither solid or liquid. Stomach muscle never tortured through a sit-up had long since atrophied. Only his skin seemed to hold his guts in.

"GPS doesn't lie."

"I know," said Roy, digging into his army surplus backpack and pulling out a two-liter bottle of Mountain Dew and a bag of pork rinds.

Jeff efficiently took his backpack off, and withdrew a black, hardened plastic case. He placed the case carefully on the ground and flipped the latches simultaneously. Jeff withdrew the thermal imager and thumbed the *on* switch to verify the battery was fully charged. Jeff had checked the battery a dozen times before they made the trip but checked it again anyway. Satisfied, he stood up and began scanning the area.

"What's with the thermal imager? Don't those things only work at night, or if Bigfoot was recently in the area?"

"True, but other things will pop up in thermal imagery. Man-made objects tend to be different temperatures than the natural surroundings. Like concrete is hotter than grass."

"So, we're good if Bigfoot dropped his lighter?"

"No. We're good if Bigfoot dropped any of the victims' equipment as he exited the area," Jeff said as he moved around a natural hedge of young hawthorns.

"Like here. This looks like where the tents were. The witnesses tried to flatten the ground to make sleeping more comfortable. The disturbed ground is evident in the infrared spectrum because it is a slightly different temperature than the rest of the ground area. Hand me a flag," Jeff said.

Roy dumped the contents of his backpack on the ground, and produced a bundle of survey flags tied together with twist ties. Jeff separated one flag free and stuck the rest in his pants pocket. He then inserted the flag in the dirt where one of the tents had been set.

"You finding any footprints?" asked Roy studying the ground.

"Nothing. The ground is fairly hard here. Maybe closer to the riverbank."

"I've got plenty of moss rubbed off of the rocks from something stepping on them, but nothing definitive."

"I'll try to isolate the individual paths each vic'

took to get to the water. Maybe that will give us a clue to where Bigfoot was standing on the bank," Roy said as he removed spools of different colored thread and began matching footprints to individuals.

"How's it coming?" Roy asked as he stomped back into the campsite. Behind him were four lines of different colored string which radiated from the campsite like spokes of a wheel. Farther down, each thread angled toward where the kayaks must have been stored, and then to the river.

"I may have a partial imprint in the soot near the campfire. The powder is so fine that it's hard to tell. It looks like somebody stepped there but only part of the foot is seen. Hard to tell how large of a foot. You?"

"I found the wrappers to the oatmeal. The victims' accounts were correct. They look like a person tore into them. I bagged them for fingerprint analysis, but I'm not too hopeful. The bags are the unbleached paper kind and are wet from the river, so I'm not sure if we'll get good prints."

"That's better than what I got, which is nothing," Jeff said, placing his hands on his waist and looking around. "I guess it's time to give Southern Tier Bigfoot Tours a call. See what they know."

9

"Creature Comforted"
~Local H

"You guys been here long?" asked Patch, hopping out of his Jeep. He could hear Earl and Harry discussing something, but he couldn't tell what the subject was.

Patch earned his nickname because he wore an eye-patch. He'd lost his left eye while playing swords made from maple branches when he was ten years old. When the accident happened, the mothers in the village leaped at the chance to make an example of him. He was the living old wives' tale of what mothers had been warning their children of since the dawn of motherhood: The Boy Who Poked His Eye Out with a Stick. He was validation for all the reproaches and admonishments dished out by mothers everywhere. Patch had been led door to door, to every child's house in the village, to show the other children what would happen if they didn't listen to their mothers. Patch's mother squeezed out every nanosecond of her fifteen minutes of fame. No sooner had the accident happened than she had reinvented herself into the role of sagely matriarch. Soon she was doling out sugared motherly advice to young mothers like a PEZ dispenser channeling Oprah.

A special event was held at the auditorium of the elementary school where Patch was paraded across the worn wooden stage, past Papier-mâché props, to be placed on display: The Living Warning. Mothers stood along the sides of the auditorium, alternately smiling smugly at one another while casting serious looks at their children seated at the spectacle.

Before Patch's loss, most of the things mothers warned their children of hadn't happened. Nobody's face froze while making faces, nobody drowned because they went swimming after eating, or caught their death from cold for running outside without a jacket, and none of the children knew anyone who grew watermelons in their bellies after swallowing watermelon seeds.

Children behaved themselves for weeks after what had become known as "The Accident". Emergency room visits were down and homework completion was up. The mothers were pleased. Across the village, mothers, mothers-in-law, grandmothers, and great-grandmothers dished out advice and warnings with renewed strength and vigor. For once, the women in the village, at least all of them with functioning uteruses, were in agreement. Pleased, indeed.

Until the patch. Because Patch was a child, glass eyes, which are made for adults, wouldn't fit into his eye socket. The only other option available was to wear an eye patch. A patch of shame to mothers; a patch of warning. But to young boys: a pirate's patch. The patch symbolized action and adventure to ten-year-olds everywhere. Patch, who until then was an unexceptional child—remarkable only in the very fact of how average he was—developed a gunslinger's swagger. He also cultivated an encyclopedic knowledge of all things pirate and nautical; despite the fact he lived several hours drive from the nearest ocean.

Patch became the bad boy of the village, in spite of the fact that he didn't do anything bad boyish. In fact, Patch had never been arrested and had only two tickets in his life; both parking. Patch enjoyed the bad boy spotlight while simultaneously avoiding the pitfalls of bad boy life, such as jail. His mother never forgave him.

"Nah, just got here," Harry replied to Patch. Harry was leaning against his truck while Earl opened the cooler in the back of the truck to fish out three beers. Patch could see several dozen empty beer cans in the bed of Harry's truck.

They were parked off a dirt road in the woods that ran along the Beaverkill River's northern edge. A Tufted Titmouse and a Hairy Woodpecker flew back and forth amongst the Eastern Hemlocks while a Black-Capped Chickadee "chica-dee-dee-de'ed" for a little feathered mate to cozy up to for the evening in the branches above their heads.

The serenity was broken when Earl resumed his monologue: "I'm telling you, we're the Romans before the Germanic tribes swooped across Europe and destroyed them," Earl flung his hand out horizontally in front of him to indicate in Earl Sign Language "swooped" but looked more like a half-assed, horizontal Nazi salute. "You want to know what I saw in the grocery store's freezer section the other day?"

"No!" Patch and Harry replied in unison, both knowing Earl would tell them anyway. Patch spun and punched Harry in the arm and yelled, "Beer!" Beer was the name of a game they all played. The rules were: if two people said something at the same time, the two people had to punch each other in the arm and say: "Beer!" The last one to land a punch owed the victor a beer. They'd been playing the game since elementary school.

"Frozen peanut butter sandwiches!" Earl

exclaimed, pausing to allow Patch and Harry time to respond in shock, or make an exclamation. Anything to indicate they too shared Earl's disbelief. None came. Earl tried again, "Frozen peanut-fuckin'-butter sandwiches inside little pie crusts!"

Patch and Harry both lifted their eyebrows in the international symbol of "So?"

"What I want to know is: who is too lazy to go through a McDonald's drive-thru?" Earl demanded. "If you don't have time to make a sandwich, you go to a fast-food restaurant! That's why they were invented! That's why I didn't join the rat race. I could get a corporate job, but that's what will happen to you. They keep you so busy you don't have time for fast food. That's no way to live, man."

Patch and Harry just stood watching Earl with matching nonplussed expressions on their face.

"You know what else I saw on the news? They're making sliced peanut butter; like the individually wrapped cheese you get from the grocery store. Now what I want to know is: who can't spread peanut butter?" Earl finished his rant by miming someone struggling to spread peanut butter, using an imaginary knife in his right hand while his left hand played the role of a slice of bread. Earl ended the dramatization by throwing down his imaginary knife and bread and exclaiming: "Oh, just fuck it!" in a mock-effeminate voice.

"So, how's Domino"? Patch asked turning toward Harry. Domino Chipotle was Harry's girlfriend.

"Not good. She's so pissed at me she can only communicate with me by speaking in song lyrics."

"She's only speaking in song lyrics?" Patch echoed, cocking his head to the side.

"Yeah, it's this thing she does. I don't understand

48

it. It's like she gets so upset she can't verbalize her feeling so she speaks in song lyrics. It took a while for me to figure out what she was doing. I made the connection when she repeated a lyric to a song I knew."

"So, it's kind of like speaking in tongues, but she's possessed by the spirit of a jukebox?"

"Yeah," Harry said, smiling at Patch. "It's really helpful sometimes. I can tell how upset she is and the mood she's in by the band she quotes. One time it was nothing but Nora Jones; she just moped around acting melancholy. Another time it was Collective Soul and she was hopeful; more kitten than tiger. I think she wanted to empower me to reach my full relationship potential. In retrospect, the Collective Soul phase was nice. One time it was Paul Westerberg, another time it was Nirvana. One time she did duets by Billie Holiday and Louis Armstrong. I liked that one. The worst she ever called me during that fight was 'Rascal' and she cooked soul food all week. One time she did nothing but Paul Simon; she kept telling me she was going to Graceland, and I could call her 'Al.' The worst was when she spoke nothing but Scott H. Biram lyrics for two weeks; I was afraid to sleep."

"Who's she doing now?"

"Tool"

"Ouch"

"Yep"

"Okay freaks, whose turn is it to get in the suit?" asked Earl, taking out an old sea bag out of the cab of his truck and placing it on the ground.

"I think it's mine. When are we going to get the new suit?" replied Patch

"It's already ordered. I got an authentic Chewbacca costume," said Earl.

"Which version?" asked Harry.

"The movie version!"

"Which movie version?"

Earl stared blankly at Harry.

"Yeah, Chewbacca's hair was kinda slicked back in Star Wars. Then it became progressively shaggier and feathered through the sequels."

"I think Princess Leia wanted him to have bangs," said Patch.

"Really? I thought he was acting out by not grooming himself as well because Han Solo was always chasing after Princess Leia. He was jealous of her. I don't think he'd let her give him bangs."

"I always thought he didn't groom himself as well because he and Han had steady jobs with the Rebel Alliance. He didn't need to look as clean-cut because they weren't pimping out the Millennium Falcon anymore."

"Are you two done?" asked Earl.

"Not yet. Does the suit come with the bandolier and wookie-purse?"

"Yes," said Earl, drawing out the monosyllabic word for three syllables.

"Okay, I'm done. No, wait. I'm not. What the hell is that smell?"

"That's my new cologne: *Le Ultra Stud eau de toilette pour homme* for men. It's made from a prize winning thoroughbred's urine and the first menstrual cycle of Malaysian girls."

"It smells like shit . . . wait, it has what in it?"

"Prize winning thoroughbred urine and the first menstrual cycle of Malaysian girls."

"You're wearing horse piss and tampon tea?"

"Sandalwood is its base note" Earl replied.

10

"The Rub"
~Porchsleeper

There are over 7,600 professional Elvis impersonators in the United States. Of those 7,600, less than 2% are Indian. Indian from India, not Native American Indian. Less than 1% of Elvis impersonators are Native American. Sheriff Flan "The King" Paan was the former: Indian from India. A loose distinction because he was born in the United States.

Flan believed he was Elvis Aaron Presley incarnate. A reincarnation impossibility considering Flan was born in 1970 and Elvis died the summer of 1977. Flan believed Elvis died in 1970, during one of Elvis's mysterious disappearances. Specifically, when Elvis showed up unannounced at the White House, was brought in to the Oval Office, and introduced to President Richard Nixon. The same meeting where Elvis presented Nixon a gold Colt .45 ACP handgun engraved with images of Elvis's life and seven silver bullets. Possibly the only person to ever bring a concealed weapon into the Oval Office without the Secret Service's knowledge, and live to tell about it.

However, some conspiracy theorists believe Elvis didn't live to tell about it, and the Secret Service's record remains untarnished. They believe Elvis was gunned down by Secret Service agents while drawing the weapon, and an impostor took his place.

Two months later, Flan's mother conceived Flan, backstage at an Elvis concert, with a man who strongly resembled the King. Flan's biological father was the world's first Elvis impersonator. Eastern religion meets pop American culture and drinks the delusional Kool-Aid.

As far as Julian Lennon impersonators, there is exactly one: Deputy Winston O'Boogie[1].

"We can't go on together with suspicious minds[2]," said Sheriff Flan Paan as he hung up the phone. Turning towards Deputy O'Boogie, "That was SUNY ESF (State University of New York College of Environmental Science and Forestry). The school is placing a missing persons report for one of their biologists: a Mr. Ian King. King- I like that name. Anyway, seems this ol' boy has been trompin' around the woods 'round here and fell down a rabbit hole. Them rangers at the Department of Environmental Conservation are playing lead singer in this investigation. We're just part of the band."

"Why are we being called then?" asked Deputy O'Boogie.

"Well, seems like Mr. King's projected route would have taken him right by town. The man was out tracking wolves by his lonesome. It was probably the wolves that got 'im. Winston, check out this ol' hound dog, and find out what you can. I'll head out to see if anyone heard anything. I'm expecting a fax from SUNY-ESF of Mr. King's planned route. Not that it should help much. He was following the wolves, and I don't think they cared much for his opinion on what

---

[1] Winston O'Boogie was a pseudonym used by John Lennon.
[2] "Suspicious Minds", written by Mark James, aka Francis Zambon.

route to take. The fax will have Mr. King's locations from when he called in his reports. That'll put us in the ballpark."

"You got it."

"And Winston, find out if any of those wolves had a tracking device on it."

Sheriff Flan swaggered into The Brown Beaver. He whisked his gold framed wraparound sunglasses of his face and tucked one ear piece into the deep 'V' of his white tunic. Squinting as his eyes adjusted to the darkened bar, he swept his gold cape beneath him and bellied up to the bar. He was careful not to lean back on the barstool, and possibly snag the rhinestone thunderbird patterned on the back.

"Hey, Cindi, can I get a Pepsi?"

"You sure, Sheriff? Isn't it about knocking off time?"

"I'm sure. Got a phone call today and I'm all shook up[3]. You hear anything about a biologist coming through town tracking wolves?"

"No. Sorry. I would've remembered something like that. Why? What's going on?"

"Hmm. Nothing to worry your pretty little head about."

Cindi blushed a little, "You coming to karaoke tomorrow night, Flan?"

"I got my hi-fi high, and the lights down low[4]."

---

[3] "All Shook Up", written by Otis Blackwell.
[4] "I Need Your Love Tonight", written by Sid Wayne and Bix Reichner.

11

"Rebel, Rebel"
~David Bowie

Domino walked into The Voodoo Lounge and Martini Bar, and glanced around the room. Retro jazz-fusion music played, softly enriching the atmosphere. She saw Echo at the other end of the bar. Domino gave a little wave, and worked her way through the after-work crowd, careful to not make eye contact with any single men. She was meeting Echo, and she really wasn't in the mood to be hit on by some drunk. The women exchanged hugs; genuine hugs, not the animatronic embrace of the ambivalent. Domino glided into the stool next to Echo.

The Voodoo Lounge was made of reclaimed wood from an old barn, and offered 201 different martinis. Domino liked it because the music was played at a volume which allowed the patrons to hold a conversation without yelling, and there was not one TV on. Unlike the Beaver, where every sporting event played in America glared at her from the 12 TVs, and classic rock thundered so loudly she would lose her voice from trying to talk.

Domino glanced under the bar at the thick wooden beam which was now the bar's footrest. She slung off her purse, and placed it on the beam to keep it off the floor. "I saw your piece on Milo Backwater."

"Ungh. I don't want to talk about it. How's Harry?"

"Good. He's the same," Domino said, trailing off.

"Uh oh. What's up, girl?"

"I don't know. I'm getting the feeling that this is it with him. You know? That this is the best he's going to be. He's not interested in the relationship going anywhere. He just wants to hang out. It's frustrating."

"How did you meet Harry?"

"In college. He was in a band, The Narcoleptic Tongues, that played all the frat parties. So, I saw him everywhere. He was a poli-sci major, and we had a few classes together. I got to know him. He was really cool back then. I mean, they were rock stars on campus. The Tongues used to play a slow-dance set at every show, and they would get the whole place to dance. Harry had this great monologue about grabbing someone, anyone, just to feel the love. The monologue always ended with a really clever sexual innuendo. One night, he pulled me up on stage, and sang Cheap Trick's "I Want You to Want Me" to me in front of everyone while we slow danced. He slung his guitar behind his back; he looked like a god. A really grungy god, but I was hooked."

"That's really sweet."

"It was the most romantic thing ever done for me. Even when I found out he was such a stoner that he didn't remember doing it."

"And the rest is history?"

"No. Yes. I don't know. The relationship has never gone anywhere. He's still wants to be that guy. He's stunted the relationship's maturity. Now I want other things: to settle down, buy a house, have kids."

"Harry doesn't want those things?"

"He says he does. He just isn't proactively working towards them. I think he wants those things as long as it doesn't get in the way of drinking beer and sex. In a weird way, I envy him. He's content. He doesn't need more from people or from me. I used to feel bad because I was asking so much from him."

"I can see Harry wanting to be a father someday."

"I can too. He gets excited about it. I'm not sure if he realizes they come out as infants. I think he thinks they come out as frat boys."

"You're an awesome person, Domino. You shouldn't feel guilty for wanting more. You have your master's, you're a therapist. You have a great job. You deserve all of those things. You aren't his groupie anymore."

"Thanks. I know. I love him, but I'm afraid he'll never change. He'll hang out with Earl and Patch for the rest of his life."

"How did he meet Patch?"

"Harry and Patch grew up together, went to college together, in the same bands; Patch is like his soul mate.

"Patch went to college?"

"Oh yeah. Patch graduated at the top of his class. He has a master's degree in Botany. He's never used it for anything but growing weed."

"At least his education didn't go to waste. Earl went to college, too?

"Nah. Not Earl. Earl thinks he knows more than anyone, so no one can teach him anything."

Domino reached across the bar, and plucked up two menus. "Enough chitchat. How far are we going to get tonight?" Domino and Echo had a goal to drink every martini the Voodoo Lounge made.

"All the way, girlfriend. Oh, oh, oh! Look! A couple on a date. We can play the game!" Echo squealed, clapping her hands.

"Where? Oh, there. Okay. Who do you want to be?" Echo and Domino's drinking game of choice was: *Here's What I'm Really Thinking.* The game was to ad-lib imaginary conversation for people in the bar.

"I'll be the guy, babe," Echo said, imitating a masculine baritone and laughing.

"Umm, okay. I'll be, like, the girl, I guess . . ." Domino responding as a California, beach bimbo.

Both women erupted into laughter, and hugged each other.

12

"Nice Guys Don't Get Paid"
~Soul Asylum

A lone man dressed completely in black stood at the edge of a natural clearing overlooking a small wooded valley. No birds could be heard chirping or seen flying from tree to tree. All the animals were avoiding the area. The man did not react to the sound of a black sedan driving down an adjacent logging trail. He also did not react to the sound of approaching footsteps carving through the short brush.

"Report," said the tallest Dark Agent without turning to face his colleagues.

"Two instigators from the Sasquatch Research Organization are in the area investigating a Bigfoot sighting made by four campers. The campers have already been interviewed by a local newsperson, Echo Clyne."

"And?"

"We sanitized the campsite of evidence before the SRO could get there. The instigators won't find anything useful."

"What of the interview?"

"The news station's general manager, Mangrove Slimebucket has been contacted and is most cooperative. We left him with the distinct impression his station would be closed down, and he would be personally fined by the FCC if the interview ever aired. We also collected all footage of the interview, as well as the editing computer's hard drive."

"What of the newscaster?"

"We have not made contact with Ms. Clyne at this time. Mr. Slimebucket assures us he will be able to keep her on a leash.

"Pay a visit to this girl and make sure she understands. Help her keep her journalistic impulse to provide what she may believe is the truth under control."

"As you wish."

"Gentlemen, for over two thousand years, we have been the ones who have safeguarded the secrets of the world. Governments and empires, religions and ideologies have risen and fallen during our watch. We alone determine what is known and who shall know it." Turning to face his colleagues for the first time. "Now, where is that fucking monkey?"

13

"To a Sucker"
~The Blacks

Harry tried to make his way towards the road in the costume. His effort was hampered by the fact he was walking across uneven terrain in a modified gorilla costume and drywaller's stilts.

"I'm going to break my neck on these stilts," Harry said into the Fisher Price walkie-talkie.

Earl's voice crackled through the toy radio. "You are only one foot high. You can't break your neck from that high."

"No?"

"No. It's all physics. You need to fall from an altitude of at least twice your own height to break your neck."

"That's bullshit."

"It's not. I fall down drunk all of the time, and I've never broken my neck. My uncle used to fall a lot before he refined his knot tying technique. Never broke anything. Got weird things stuck in him, but never broke any bones. Until he decided to do it from the second floor balcony of his house. He said he liked to enjoy the view while he worked. Anyway, the rope snapped and he landed on the concrete porch below. When the sheriff investigated, he had fallen from exactly double his height plus one inch."

"Are you fucking serious?"

"Yeah, but that isn't the weird part. The weird part is he landed directly onto a broom handle. Right up his ass. Fucking killed him. He must've been sweeping cobwebs while dangling himself from that rope. He was really particular about his brooms. Had to have a certain handle. He may have been allergic to different woods or varnishes. I don't know."

"Didn't your uncle borrow this suit?"

"Yeah. He needed it for a costume party. That's why there's a tear in the ass of the costume. He said a dog attacked him in the suit. He's the one who got the yogurt stains all over it."

"We need a new suit."

Patch's voice crackled over the radios. "A car is coming! A minivan. Looks like a soccer mom with her kids."

"I'm on my way." Harry started moving quickly down towards the road. Gravity and his own momentum took over and Harry began running towards the road to keep from face-planting. Harry hit the road at a full gallop as the minivan rounded the bend. Winning the speed battle but losing the balance war, Harry stumbled into a headfirst dive midway across the road.

Inside the minivan, Jasmine Dickover was disgusting herself as she sang along with the Wiggles for her twins, Wayne and Jane.

"Mommmmmmmeeeeeeeeeee! Play the 'Fruit Salad' yummy yummy song again!"

Movement in front of the car caught Jasmine's eye. She glanced up in time to see a brown animal diving across the road directly in front of her.

Thump!

"Mommy ran over a monkey!"

14

"I Was Wrong"
~Social Distortion

A black sedan sat across the street from a building in the downtown area of the village. Nearly every building downtown was cataloged in the National Historic Registry. The streets were still made of cobblestones and eighteen-wheelers were diverted around to reduce wear on the stones. Echo Clyne's apartment building was in an eighteenth century three-story walkup which had been converted into lofts and apartments. The lofts attracted young, middle-class couples, and the downtown streets were filled with cafes, bars, and art galleries.

The apartment's interior contrasted the building's antiquated exterior. The original wood floors had been ripped out and replaced with Pergo flooring. Walls had been knocked out to make the rooms larger. The entire electric systems had been rewired, and now quietly hummed with i-Pods, i-Phones, LED light fixtures, and Italian coffee machines. The architectural equivalent of giving Keith Richards a blood transfusion.

Echo Clyne upheld a strict weeknight routine. Monday through Thursday nights, she made herself a small, organic meal followed by forty-five minutes on the treadmill. After, she would quickly shower and then surf the couch into a sea of reality television until midnight.

Two men dressed identically in black suits sat in

the front seat of the sedan. "She's on the treadmill. She's gone through her warm up and is now running at max. We have approximately 30 minutes," said one agent. He stared forward through the sedan's front windshield. He was not speaking to his partner. Both agents had miniature earpieces in their ears. Nearly invisible, the earpieces camouflaged themselves to the wearer's skin color exactly. The camouflage matched skin color, but did adequately approximate the shadow of the wearer's ear canal. To an outside observer, each agent appeared to have a shallow ear canal–both in the right ear.

The voice of the tallest Dark Agent filled both agents' right ear. "Put the fear of god into her."

Echo had 15 minutes left of her run. To fight the boredom of running on a treadmill, she solved equations in her head. Breaking the time, speed, and distance into fractions. Then calculating how far she would travel in the remaining time, how far she had already run, how many feet she ran in each minute, how many footsteps did she take to run a mile, etc.

She was so focused on solving the math problems in her head, she did not hear the soft motorized whirring sound of the electronic lock pick being used on the other side of her apartment door. Nor did she hear the dead bolt click into the unlock position. The agent timed that perfectly to happen with one of her footfalls on the treadmill.

She did hear the two agents burst through the door. Echo's head jerked back to the left at the sound of the two agents coming in. Later, she would have trouble recalling the sound of the agents made themselves, just the sound of the door banging open. Twisting her body mid-stride on the treadmill, Echo lost her rhythm. Her feet were quickly pulled behind her on the treadmill's belt as her upper body pitched forward. Her temple slammed on an electronic heart-rate handle. As she fell, her right foot caught on the post of the right handrail, keeping her body from being pushed entirely off the back of the treadmill. Instead, her body crumbled and rolled off the right side of the treadmill on to an army surplus bag.

15

"Ain't Gonna Suck Itself"
~Cracker

"What else ya got?" Ted asked, looking across the table at Don. Don was the asylum's resident Inappropriate Public Masturbator. Ted was still in the barfly persona. His voice sounded like he'd been taking whiskey shots out of a dirty ashtray.

Don leaned over the game table and assumed a conspiratorial tone, "I got Viagra."

"What? How'd you get Viagra?"

"They give 'em to me," Don said, nodding towards a nurse on the other side of the break room. "It's part of my treatment."

"The state gives a chronic masturbator boner pills?"

"They're for my self-esteem."

"What?" Ted asked, carefully laying his Uno cards down on the table. He stared in disbelief at the sweaty, fat man with the worst comb-over on the planet sitting across from him. "Don, I'm not sure if an erection will help."

Don also laid his cards on the table, carefully blocking anyone from seeing their face value. "Erectile dysfunction is a serious issue which leaves an indelible mark on my psyche, and my feeling of self-worth as a man."

"But you act inappropriately when you have a boner."

"Hey, you're infringing on my basic human right to

masturbate. There's nothing wrong with self-love. I can't get better until my self-esteem improves, and I can't get better self-esteem if I cannot function as a man. What you call 'inappropriate' is my way of accepting and loving myself, for who I am. Masturbation also releases stress."

"I wish that's all it would release."

"You are a prude, Ted."

"Whatever, Captain Jack[5]."

"Yeah, whatever, Dear Prudence[6]."

"Right. Just play the game, monkey spanker." Ted picked his hand back up. "And wash your hands before you play anymore games."

Don turned towards Lyle, the Catatonic Cardinal of Rigid Flexibility. Lyle was given the nickname by one of the orderlies because he shifted between the rigid posture commonly associated with catatonics and catatonic excitement. When Lyle shifted into catatonic excitement, he flailed his limbs around excitedly. It was unnerving to see a man sit in one position for hours without moving to jumping around like he had ants in his pants. It was like his body was trying to shake his muscles awake, or maybe he sat still because his muscles were exhausted. Nobody really knew which, but they all knew Lyle had the best pills.

"Whatcha got there, Lyle?" Don asked, pawing at Lyle's pill pile. "Oooooo, Thorazine. Thorazine gives me the shakes. They're great for my self-esteem therapy. It's like a vibrating bed." One of Don's hands snaked beneath the table and began rubbing the crotch of his pajama pants.

"Hey! Cut that shit out. I told you to do that on your own time," Ted said.

---

[5] "Captain Jack", written by Billy Joel.
[6] "Dear Prudence", written by John Lennon.

"Ted, I only need one hand to play Uno."

"No, you need both hands. C'mon, we're gambling for meds. What else does Lyle have? Never mind, I'll look myself. I don't want your dick skinners touching my winnings."

Don looked at the three people sitting at the table with a genuine hurt look. "Ted, I wash my hands before I . . ."

"La la la la la la" Ted interrupted, "I don't want to know, and you are full of shit. You are going to tell me a convulsive masturbator washes his hands first?"

"It's part of the foreplay. I'm complex."

Ted ignored Don and checked Lyle's hand. "All righty, Lyle, what'll be? I think you should go with this." Ted held a card in front of Lyle's face.

Lyle stared straight ahead.

"No? What about this?" Don held up another card for Lyle.

More staring.

"Ooooo, Lyle. You're going for the throat. Watch out boys, the shark is out."

Ted slapped a Wild Draw Four card down on the pile and turned Don "Blue."

"That's bullshit, Lyle." Don protested. He glared at the catatonic as if he'd actually played the card. "What are you betting?" Don resumed pawing through Lyle's pills. "Thorazine, Midazolam, and Prozac? Where's the good stuff?"

"Leave him alone," said Montgomery, speaking for the first time. Montgomery was Lyle's unofficial bodyguard. Catatonics can't really defend themselves, so they sometimes require a friend to look out for them. Montgomery assumed the mantle when he caught some orderlies amusing themselves one night by posing Lyle in different positions. Montgomery's punishment was swift and thoroughly ruthless. One of those orderlies ended up confined to a wheelchair in the hospital wing for the vegetables, affectionately known as the Salad Bar. The former orderly also developed a phobia of certain mental patients.

Don smiled innocently at Montgomery. Even Don avoided confronting a man who could not perceive empathy, especially a man who tended to make snow angels in the walls with an agitator's body when they pissed him off. Add Montgomery's cognitive dissidence that the wood splintering, bone cracking, and drywall dust caused by using someone's body to make snow angels might seriously hurt the snow angel.

Montgomery changed the subject but his eyes never left Don's. "I hear you see Bigfoot." Montgomery's speech pattern was slow, deep, and awkward. A certain amount of extra active-listening was required to communicate with him, especially when he stared at one person while directing his conversation towards someone else.

Ted understood the nuances of talking with Montgomery. He paused before answering. He was comfortable making up personas and manufacturing stories to go with them. The question hit closer to home. Ted wasn't ready to talk about Bigfoot. Certainly not in front of Don.

That bastard will probably start molesting himself at the thought of Bigfoot.

Don cued in on Ted's hesitation and attempted to gain favor with Montgomery. "Yeah, Ted. You're supposed to get better in the hospital. You're getting worse. Now you're having visions, or is it delusions of grandeur?" Don smirked and rolled his eyes for Montgomery. Montgomery slowly raised the corner of his upper lip. Don flinched.

The air cracked with an unfamiliar voice. "I've seen Bigfoot, too," said Lyle. Nobody had ever heard Lyle speak before.

16

"How You Like Me Now?"
~The Heavy

The billboard in front of The Brown Beaver read "Rock 'n Roll Karaoke Showdown: Julian Lennon vs. Elvis." Inside, battle lines were already drawn, with Elvis holding a clear advantage. Three heavy-set women standing in the middle of the demilitarized zone, oblivious to the growing tensions, butchered Sister Sledge's "We Are Family."

The front door opened and Sheriff Flan Paan strutted in. The bar sounds were replaced with a low rumble of drunks pseudo-whispering. Flan was dressed head to toe in black leather; Elvis's comeback outfit. Flan's mutton-chop sideburns were perfectly symmetrical. His Indian hair, sculpted into the signature pompadour, appeared blue-black against the leather. Flan had experimented to find the precise amount of hairspray which would allow his hair to fall into a wild, sexy mess midway through his set.

The karaoke DJ cut off the Sister Sledge massacre. The three women turned to complain, but were interrupted by a fierce spotlight illuminating an Indian man dressed as the King of Rock 'n Roll.

A second spotlight focused on a smaller man standing on the other end of the bar. Deputy Winston O'Boogie was dressed in jeans and a dark T-shirt. His longish, brown hair was pushed back, revealing a slightly receding hairline. A necklace of sandalwood beads completed the look. Winston rolled his eyes as

Flan pretended to karate chop a few members of the audience. He set down his drink, and walked towards the karaoke machine. His smile and nods to the audience were unassuming, even slightly self-conscience. The polar opposite to Flan's over-the-top antics and garbled, singsong, "thank-ya-very-much" flattery. The crowd parted to allow him to pass while a spotlight tracked him.

Flan ignored Winston as he approached, continuing to ham it up for the audience. He conducted psychological warfare by snubbing Winston a full minute before pretending to notice him. He struck a crowd-pleasing Elvis stance, then turned back to his supporters, and mocked his opponent some more.

The DJ walked up to stand between the two singers. Winston smiled politely, while Flan assumed a confident stance. "Ladies and gentlemen, are you ready to rock 'n roll?"

The crowd answered back enthusiastically. Winston nodded in agreement while Flan launched into more stage theatrics.

The DJ continued working the crowd: "The night we've all been waiting for. The ultimate karaoke battle: Elvis versus Julian Lennon! Each singer will sing ten songs. The opener will be determined by a coin toss." Turning towards Winston, "Julian, heads or tails?"

"Sheriff Paan can start," Winston said, throwing a passive-aggressive barb by not referring to Flan by his stage name.

"Whoa, now. The King don't open for nobody," Flan responded.

The DJ moved to stand between the singers like a referee. "Gentlemen, are you ready?"

"A little less conversation, a little more action,

please[7]," Flan said. Winston only nodded.

"Okay, ladies and gentlemen: Julian Lennon!"

Julian grabbed the mike from the stand, and gave the DJ a nod to begin. The familiar, machine gun electric guitar opening of The Beatles's "Revolution[8]" erupted from the amps. Winston howled a reasonable facsimile of Paul McCartney's cry, then launched into the first verse: "*You say you want a revolution. Well, you know, we all want to change the world.*"

Winston proved he was playing for keeps by launching into a Beatles song first. In his defense, John Lennon wrote and sang the song, and it wasn't unusual for Julian Lennon to play some of his father's songs in concert.

With the addition of some Beatles songs to Winston's set, the bar became more evenly divided between Elvis and Beatles fans. Flan ignored Winston's set while he continued to mingle with his fans.

Winston ended his set with another Beatles song, *Come Together*. When his vocals were finished, Winston gave a deep bow to the audience, his hands steepled in prayer, and returned the mic to the stand before the song ended. He gave a small wave to the crowd as he exited the stage. He smiled and talked congenially with his supporters as he made his way back to his drink.

Sheriff Paan jumped up on the stage. Eager to prove he was the better entertainer, he launched directly

---

[7] "A Little Less Conversation, written by Mac Davis and Billy Strange.

[8] "Revolution", written by John Lennon. Sometimes referred to as *Revolution 2* to distinguish it from the acoustic version of the song on the *White Album*. The electric version was issued as the "B" side of *Hey Jude*.

into "Heartbreak Hotel".

17

Calling Dr. Love

~Kiss

"Saw most beautiful She-Bigfoot in the world today! Bigfoot so excited. Bigfoot need some fresh blood in his life. Tired of She-Bigfoot around here. She-Bigfoot around here way too comfortable. No problem making comment about Bigfoot. Liked better when we don't know each other well. Everyone still polite. Bigfoot polite because want to mate with She-Bigfoot. Do whatever take. Make small talk. Take bath. Pick flower. No eat skunk for a while. Leave whiskey alone. She-Bigfoot polite because no want to mate with Bigfoot. Maybe She-Bigfoot does want mate. Who the fuck knows what She-Bigfoot want? Never figure out.

After make big mate. She-Bigfoot get comfortable with relationship. Bigfoot no like. Like Bigfoot semen stimulate bitch-gland. Not enough if Bigfoot make She-Bigfoot orgasm. Bigfoot found human magazine article - Your 12 Erogenous Zones. She-Bigfoot and human female have same erogenous zones. Who knew? Not sure about human male. Not really care. Know where Bigfoot erogenous zone is. Why we have one and female have 12? Not fair. So many zones and not want to mate. If Bigfoot have 12 erogenous zones; Bigfoot never leave den. Bigfoot play with one erogenous zone too much as it is.

Not really matter if Bigfoot give She-Bigfoot orgasm. She-Bigfoot still going to want to improve

Bigfoot. She-Bigfoot want little more. Never satisfied. Bigfoot orgasm, She-Bigfoot orgasm; good times for everyone. Not She-Bigfoot. Penetration, no matter how slight, start Bigfoot improvement cycle. Sometime, She-Bigfoot stop in middle of mate because not comfortable with relationship. Say not happy with relationship. Say relationship not going in direction She-Bigfoot want. Say no want be good-time girl. Bigfoot like good-time girl. Not see problem. Bigfoot want to stay with good-time girl. Bigfoot not want to stay with not-happy-with-relationship girl. She-Bigfoot say want Bigfoot to want She-Bigfoot. Then say not sure want serious relationship with Bigfoot. Then why bring it up with Bigfoot? Bigfoot not want to be Bigfoot of dreams, so Bigfoot okay if she not sure about serious relationship with Bigfoot. Bigfoot want to mate and not talk about it.

Once, She-Bigfoot peed in Bigfoot bed. Bigfoot no like, but Bigfoot notice She-Bigfoot no complain if She-Bigfoot embarrassed. She-Bigfoot not want to tell Bigfoot all his problem after she sleep in own piss. Try make She-Bigfoot drink lot of water before sleep. Not sleep too close.

Try not to make She-Bigfoot orgasm. Maybe if She-Bigfoot not satisfied, then no want improve Bigfoot. Not work. Want improve Bigfoot and improve Bigfoot technique. Bigfoot no want to hear sex technique need help. She-Bigfoot penis flytrap.

Anyhoo, new She-Bigfoot skinny. Not big like other She-Bigfoot. Most She-Bigfoot big as Bigfoot. Bigfoot no like. Bigfoot say equal to or lesser than. Tired of big She-Bigfoot. Bigfoot need to watch mouth around big She-Bigfoot. One She-Bigfoot kick Bigfoot ass. Bigfoot no like. Bigfoot only say want to mate with She-Bigfoot and She-Bigfoot friend. Not see what *problem. She-Bigfoot and friend always tickling and kissing on each other when Bigfoot find fermented apples. Bigfoot included She-Bigfoot. Not left out. She-Bigfoot punched Bigfoot right in face. All forest creatures laugh. Deer still laugh at Bigfoot. Deer fast. Bigfoot no can catch. Hope skinny She-Bigfoot no can hit hard. Why She-Bigfoot always want to hit Bigfoot?*

Only weird thing. New She-Bigfoot smell funny. Not like other She-Bigfoot. Like new She-Bigfoot bathe in perfume and horse piss."

18

"Why Don't We Get Drunk (And Screw)"
~Jimmy Buffett

Harry stumbled into Domino's kitchen. Really, he exploded into her kitchen. No knock. No doorbell. A fart squeezed out with a sneeze. He held a beer to his temple and tangled a nearly empty case of beer in the other hand. Blood was crusted in his hair and dried to his ear. On his legs were what appeared to be pants made of monkey fur. The monkey pants were covered in twigs and the inseam was far too long. Overall, he looked like the Greek god Pan after a bender.

"Oh my god! What the hell happened to you? Are you three still forcing each other through initiations to be in your club? Let me make this clear: you three are the only ones who want to be in your club so there is absolutely no need for the annual initiation," Domino said.

Harry laid his most suave look on his girlfriend and slurred "Initiations keep the riffraff out and aren't for another month." He pulled a broken cigarette from somewhere inside the monkey pants and lit the filter end.

Domino expertly smacked the smoldering cigarette out of Harry's mouth. The trajectory of her strike caused the cigarette to sail like a comet into the sink; extinguishing it with an annoyed pssssst.

"What happened then?"

A boyfriend's survival instinct should be a finely tuned early warning system. Not refined enough to pick up a woman's subtle hints, glares, and nudges. An innate energy-saving feature; only real threats initiate a fight or flight response. At the first hint of danger, threat, discussion of marriage or commitment–any feminine tools of warfare–his sympathetic nervous system blasts neurons in the *locus coeruleus*. The abundance of catecholamines at a man's neuroreceptors triggers intuitive behavior in the man.

An evolutionary double standard. A woman's intuition is always on, constantly sifting through grains of data until a connection is made.

A man's intuition defaults to standby. Oblivious to even the most glaring clues. Then hyper-stimulated adrenal glands fork his tongue and squeeze his bullshit gland. He'll start blabbing any word combination he thinks will extinguish the threat, make her happy, or get her to stop being mad.

Unfortunately Harry's early warning system was as drunk as he was. If it wasn't, his spidey-sense would have been tingling.

"Who wants to make the sex?"

"What?"

"Who wants to make the sex?" Harry repeated as he began pulling down the monkey pants. He attempted to chase her out of the kitchen with his own personal spear leading the charge. Tripping over the pile of monkey pants around his ankles, he caught himself on the counter and leaned on the Formica surface.

"Want to play slap and tickle?"

Sliding down off the counter, he sat on the floor, and began pulling the monkey pants off.

"Harry! What happened to your foot?"

"Nothin'. So what color panties do you have on?"

"Harry, your foot is black-and-blue!"

Pulling himself up the counter. "Are you wearing black and blue panties?"

She shoved him back down to the floor. He tried to pull her down on top of him. Domino twisted away and kicked him in the foot.

"Yoooooowwwwwwwwwwwwwww!"

"Awwwww. What happened to your little erection?"

"Don't call it 'little.'"

"Shut up, you. Now tell me what happened to your foot."

"I can't shut up and tell you about my foot . . ."

Domino cocked her leg back to deliver another kick.

"Okay, okay. I was hit by a car at work."

"You don't have a job!"

"I do. Patch, Earl, and I started our own company."

"Oh for fuck's sake . . . what kind of company did you three 'tards start?"

"A Bigfoot tour company."

"A what? I'm sorry. It sounded like you said something about Bigfoot. I didn't hear anything after that because nothing could possibly be intelligent after the word 'Bigfoot.'"

"I said: 'a Bigfoot tour company.' Southern Tier Bigfoot Tours."

"Bigfoot doesn't exist! How can you give a tour of something that doesn't exist?"

"That's the beauty! We create Bigfoot! Ample opportunity for growth! Buy low, sell high. The sky's the limit. Shatter the glass ceiling. The market is wide open! Speaking of wide open . . ."

Domino cocked her foot back again. "Keep talking."

"Okay. Check this out. We hoax Bigfoot, right? Generate some buzz about Bigfoot sightings in the area. Then, we sell tours. We take people out to where the Bigfoot sightings were."

"Let me get this straight. You are dressing up like Bigfoot to sell tours?"

"Not just dress up. That's too short sighted. We hoax everything! Footprints, hair samples, photographs, vocalizations, stool samples; plus actual sightings by our good neighbors! We are creating sightings of Bigfoot and people are reporting it to the sheriff. They're blogging about it, posting it on Facebook. Free advertising! We create the supply and the demand!"

"Then what?"

"Then people come to our website. We offer trips to take people out to the sightings."

"How much are you charging?"

"$200 per person for a day tour and $500 per person to camp overnight in Bigfoot country."

"What's to stop people from coming up here and camping without paying you?"

"Nothing, but we know where the Bigfoot sightings are, so it's cost-prohibitive not to go with us."

"Does Bigfoot ever show up to these tours?"

"Nope. Also part of the beauty. We offer no guarantee and no refunds if Bigfoot doesn't show."

Domino stared at him intently, wrinkling the space between her eyebrows.

"Well?"

"I can't decide if it's ingenious or idiotic."

"All the best plans are."

"No. Only all of your plans are."

"My foot still hurts. Can you kiss it?"

Domino bent down and tenderly kissed his ankle.

"You know, Chinese acupuncturists knew the meridian for the feet was located on the tip of a man's penis. If you really wanted my foot to feel better, you'd kiss there."

"You aren't Chinese," Domino said as she took his beer and walked out of the kitchen. She stopped in the doorway and turned around to face him. "Did you say you hoaxed Bigfoot pooh?"

"Yeah! Want to hear about it?"

"No and you aren't allowed to make Bigfoot pooh in my house."

19

"A Hard Rain's A-Gonna Fall"
~Bob Dylan

Echo slowly became aware of voices behind her. Recalling a women's self-defense piece she'd worked; she remained still and began mentally surveying her surroundings. She could hear one man speaking. She remembered two men had come in. Where was the other one? He wasn't responding to the talker. The talker must be on a cell phone. He was briefing someone on their status. She'd done enough break-in pieces to know they weren't coordinated by someone outside.

What the fuck is going on?

She began assessing where she was. She knew she was still in her apartment. She could hear the sound of the treadmill running directly behind her. The gentle vibrations of the belt running confirmed her theory. That meant she was wedged between the treadmill and the wall. Beside . . . beside her dad's hunting bag. Echo's left hand was pinned underneath her. She cautiously moved her fingers. She felt the rough fabric of the bag beneath her. Mentally, she inventoried what was in the pack. Was the pistol in it? She wasn't sure, but she knew there would be a hunting knife.

She stretched her fingers to feel for the zipper. She felt a seam and then the teeth of the zipper. Slowly, she began walking her fingers along the zipper's teeth; searching for the pull tab. She reminded herself to breathe. How did a knocked-out person breathe? Like they were asleep?

Her finger touched a piece of metal: the pull tab. She tried to pull the tab with her fingernail. The tab slipped from under her nail and softly clicked against the teeth of the zipper. The talker paused mid-sentence. He must have heard that. Echo waited until the talker resumed his conversation. This time she pinched the tab between her pointer and bird finger and slowly pulled.

Echo began mentally taking notes of everything that happened. She listened to the talker. Did he have an accent? Not at all. He spoke in short clipped sentences. No fluff or banter. Like a military person. She still didn't hear the second man.

She managed to unzip enough to squeeze her hand into the bag. To avoid moving her arm, she twisted her wrist uncomfortably to get better access. Inside the bag, she felt around for the leather sheath of the knife or leather holster of the pistol. In her way was a large can, like a can of spray paint. Echo tried to feel underneath the can for leather. Her arm was falling asleep from lying on it. *What the hell is the can for?* Then she remembered. *It will have to do.*

The talker seemed to be wrapping up his phone call.

She moved her fingers along the can until she felt the trigger mechanism. She grabbed the can firmly, ensuring her index finger was on the trigger and waited for her cue.

"I'll report back when she wakes up," said the talker.

Echo quickly sat up, pulling the can of bear spray out of the bag in one clean motion. Bear spray is not the same as pepper spray. Pepper spray can fit on a key ring or even be as small as a ring. Bear spray comes in a large can which pumps a higher concentrated spray than that intended for a human. The main ingredient of both pepper spray and bear spray is an extract of red pepper oil–Oleoresin Capsicum (OC) which affects the upper respiratory system, triggering involuntary eye closure and intense burning. The active ingredient in pepper spray is capsaicin, which is a chemical derived from chilies. It is the capsaicin–and related capsaicinoids–that are the active ingredients in bear spray.

The big difference is heat. A Jalapeno pepper is rated at 2,000 to 8,000 SHU (Scoville Heat Units). Pepper spray is rated at 25,000 SHU. Bear spray is rated at 2,000,000 SHU.

Both men spun around at the sound of her movement. She aimed the spray at their faces and pulled the trigger with such force that she broke through the plastic safety tab and trigger mechanism. There was no way to stop the spray. It would discharge until it was empty.

Both men went down. Their faces blistering and swelling. Echo smoothly got to her feet and moved towards the kitchen as she continued to direct the spray at both men. Her cell phone was on the kitchen table next to a black bag that was not hers. She picked up her cell phone and dialed 911. As she spoke to the operator, she directed the last of the spray towards the kitchen smoke detector. The smoked detector began chirping shrilly. The volume and frequency of the smoke alarm set off the glass break sensors of the apartment's alarm system. Simultaneously, the alarm company was signaled of the break-in. Echo's home phone rang.

"This is Fortress Security . . "

"Two men have broken into my apartment! Send

the sheriff immediately!" Echo interrupted. She tossed the phone down and went for her desk.

One of the men pulled himself off the floor using the couch as leverage. Blinded, he tried to wipe his face on his sleeve; smearing the bear spray deeper into his skin. He bent over, and reached for the sound of his partner vomiting. He grabbed his partner's collar and began pulling him towards the door.

Echo reached her desk and grabbed a futuristic-looking weapon. She thumbed the safety as she aggressively approached the two men. Projecting cool confidence as she held the police-issue X26 Taser in a classic self-defense stance. She rounded the couch with a smooth sidestep. Keeping constant focus on her assailants. Both men were vomiting now. One was dragging the other towards the front door. Blinded by the bear spray, they weren't making very good progress.

The standing agent froze at the sound of Echo's footsteps. They weren't the spastic footsteps of a frightened women running away. These were the confident footsteps of an aggressor. He spun towards the sound and forced one watery eye open. The burning was excruciating, but he immediately recognized the Taser and involuntarily raised his arm in defense. Echo's index finger squeezed the trigger. Two darts trailing wires shot from the Taser. The darts, six inches apart, hit the standing man's chest. Current flowed through the wires to the darts and he lost all muscular control. Grunting involuntarily through clenched teeth, his body convulsed in spasm in her doorway.

As he raised his hand, Echo noticed an angry scar in the middle of his palm. As he fell to the floor, she saw the other hand did as well.

Echo ejected the spent cartridge and moved back towards the desk for a new cartridge. She grabbed the cartridge and locked it into place on the X26. Satisfied the cartridge was seated correctly, she ran back towards the men.

As she rounded the corner the second time, both men were gone. She entered the landing and looked over the railing. From this vantage, she could see the entire stairwell. Nothing.

20

"Love Removal Machine"
~The Cult

"I don't know why humans bother looking for Bigfoot. Why bother Bigfoot all time? Bigfoot just want peace and quiet. Bigfoot no come hunt people! Bigfoot no care what human doing. Bigfoot no want study human. Bigfoot no take human specimen. Well, Bigfoot not take specimen anymore. Human female make too much noise. All human female want to do is scream. Worse than She-Bigfoot. Anyway, human ever notice no forest animal come study human?

How you like Bigfoot come to subdivision? Put up hunting camera on cul de sac? Take picture of human while human trying to take shit. Bigfoot need privacy! Already have bear watching. No need human watching too. Maybe Bigfoot find you in human natural habitat. Chase you around strip mall, make you spill coffee. How you like that?

Bigfoot hunters bunch of geeks who screw up Bigfoot weekend. Every Thursday, Bigfoot hunters come and make noise until Sunday. Bigfoot only get Monday, Tuesday, and Wednesday for peace. It like Bigfoot in custody battle for own home! Geeks come to woods and lay traps for Bigfoot. Is that what humans do to each other? You leave snare for neighbor?

Geeks wander around woods and bang rocks together and bang sticks on logs. Like that supposed to attract Bigfoot! You see any other animal come when people make a bunch of noise. You see Bambi run up to join the fun? That no attract Bigfoot. Bigfoot throw rock at geeks to scare away. It Saturday morning! Bigfoot try to sleep in. Bigfoot throw rock at geeks and geeks take rock home to study it. Geeks can stick rock up ass as long as be quiet.

And what with recording? Geeks play recording of baby crying, different animal calls, aborigine. That never going work. Bigfoot bachelor. No care about baby crying. That might attract She-Bigfoot. Give She-Bigfoot maternal instinct. Make She-Bigfoot frustrated with Bigfoot. She-Bigfoot want some direction in relationship. Want to know relationship going someplace. Say she getting older. Say heartbroken so many time. Like that Bigfoot fault! She say not sure Bigfoot make good father. Then why bring up want baby with Bigfoot? Bigfoot no bring up baby with She-Bigfoot. Bigfoot avoid conversation at all cost. Then geek show up with crying baby soundtrack. So Bigfoot no get sleep and She-Bigfoot frustrated with relationship. Happens every weekend. It like bad Groundhog Day. Why geeks do this to Bigfoot? And why a baby crying? What make human think everyone care about baby crying? What, every human lose mind when hear baby crying? Geeks."

21

"Battleship Chains"
~Georgia Satellites

Sheriff Flan "The King" Paan scanned Echo's apartment. They both sat in her living room. He in a chair facing Echo, she on the couch with a cup of tea. He eyed her. She wasn't acting shaken up. Everyone handled stress differently; many succumbed to the aftershock of the situation. Not Echo. She was cool.

"How'd you happen to have a police-issue Taser in your apartment?"

"I did an expose' on non-lethal self-defense. One of the dealers I interviewed gave it to me."

"Tasers are illegal in New York. Under the circumstances I'm not going to arrest you, but I am going to confiscate the weapon."

"What about the bear spray?"

"Well, your Daddy bought bear spray approved for sale in New York. You aren't supposed to use it on humans, but you didn't break any laws. How did you know to spray the smoke detector?"

"My sister and I used to have hair spray fights when we were kids. We were spraying each other under the smoke detector one day, and it went off. Then I read one day that it was the way to test smoke detectors. I knew the smoke detector would set off the glass-break alarm because it's happened before when I burned something in the oven. It all just came to me."

"Well, there's a-whole lotta shakin' goin' on[9]. That was pretty slick, darlin'."

Satisfied with the interview. Sheriff Paan excused himself to continue his investigation. He entered the kitchen and donned gloves to examine the black bag. Echo followed him into the kitchen and moved to the opposite side of the table. Sheriff Paan looked at the bag and sighed. The bag was black leather and shaped like a rectangle. Like the cases some people carried their bibles in. Sheriff Paan carefully unzipped the bag and opened it. Inside was a neatly arranged intravenous injection kit. There was one vial in the kit underneath an elastic retaining band. Sheriff Paan pushed the vial with a ballpoint pen to read the label.

"Sodium Thiopental."

"Is that like Sodium Pentothal?" asked Deputy O'Boogie, entering the kitchen with a fingerprint dusting kit.

"They are the same thing. Sodium Pentothal is a brand name for Sodium Thiopental."

"Truth serum? Why would these guys have truth serum?" asked Echo.

"Maybe they were going to interrogate you?" asked Deputy O'Boogie.

"Maybe that's not what these boys had in mind. Sodium Thiopental is also used for compliance. It weakens resolve and can make people more open to suggestion," replied Sheriff Paan. He stared up at the ceiling and blew out his cheeks. "Winston, what did you find dusting for fingerprints?"

"Not good. I got the rub marks made by fingers touching the doorknobs, but no fingerprints. Looks like they had their finger tips removed."

---

[9] "Whole Lotta Shakin' Going On", written by Dave "Curlee" Williams.

"I gotta hunka, hunka burning[10] bad feeling about this."

Deputy O'Boogie couldn't get his head around how the two intruders disappeared so fast. He suggested Echo reenact her story from when she tased the intruder to their vanishing act. He and Sheriff Paan acted as the intruders as Echo retraced her steps through the apartment. Her reenactment took less than ten seconds. Not much time for them to get down the stairs and out the door. Not without Echo hearing.

Stepping out onto the landing between apartments. Sheriff Paan and Deputy O'Boogie peered over the railing. The entire common area was visible from this vantage point. The wrought iron railings along the stairs offered zero blind areas for concealment. Sheriff Paan glanced at Echo's next-door neighbors' door. He knocked on the door and announced, "Sheriff's Department."

"They aren't home. They always come in later on Thursday nights. I think they may go to counseling," Echo offered.

Sheriff Paan nodded to Deputy O'Boogie. "Dust the door knob."

Sheriff Paan's pistol caught her eye. It was a gold-plated Colt .45 ACP. "Pretty flashy gun for law enforcement."

A lopsided smile appeared on the sheriff's face. "Yes, ma'am. It was one of Elvis'. The King had Colt make 300 commemorative WWII pistols. All engraved with different scenes of Elvis's life. Elvis used this particular gun to shoot a television."

---

[10] "Burning Love", written by Dennis Linde.

"Why did he shoot the TV?"

"Robert Goulet was on television."

"And he said something Elvis didn't like?"

"He did.   It was nothing personal.   Elvis was always shooting televisions. His basement was filled with boxes of new televisions. Elvis would shoot a TV and one of his handlers would bring him up a new one."

"Sounds expensive."

"Not for a King."

"I got the same prints," Deputy O'Boogie called out, backing away from the door.

Both men drew their side arms.   Sheriff Paan checked the doorknob. It was unlocked. He nodded to Deputy O'Boogie and entered the apartment. Investigation would prove no obvious break-in and nothing missing. The only evidence that someone had been there was a small puddle of vomit in the kitchen and the patio door leading to the fire escape was wide open.

Sheriff Paan returned to Echo standing on the landing between apartments. "Here's my card with my cell number. If you remember anything else, please give me a call."

"There was one thing. One man had scars on both hands."

"What kind of scars?"

"Crucifixion scars."

22

"I Wanna Be Your Dog"
~The Stooges

"All right, freaks, we got the new suit," Earl said stepping out of his truck. He opened the rear cab door and pulled out a large cardboard box and tossed the box into the bed of the truck. He stepped back, making room for Harry and Patch.

Patch and Earl stepped up to the truck to examine the box. "Fetish Costume Emporium? You got the costume from a sex shop? What is wrong with you?" Patch asked.

"I did a Google search. This was the cheapest costume. I don't care where it came from," replied Earl.

"Better not be used."

"It's brand-new."

"Chewbacca is a fetish? People are fucking weird," said Harry.

"That's nothing. For every person in the world, there's a fetish: midgets, amputees, cripples, farting, robots, animal sex, chubby-chasers. You name it. You can buy school girls' used underwear out of vending machines in Japan. There's no limit to what gets people's jello quivering. Whatever you are, someone is into it. Find a chick that's been horribly burned; there's a dude out there who's into that. Chewbacca is fairly tame compared to some things."

"You're saying a large, hairy, nonhuman, biped fetish is fairly tame."

"I'm saying when compared to people who are turned on by smelling farts . . ."

"Human farts, right?"

"Yeah."

"Chewbacca isn't human. So wanting sex with a hairy alien is okay but . . ."

"Eproctophilia," said Patch.

"What's that?" asked Earl.

"Eproctophilia is the name of the fart fetish."

"I'm not going to ask how you know that."

"I knew this girl . . ."

"You knew a girl who had farts you were into?"

"She was into mine."

"Shut the fuck up."

"Dude, she was!"

"Bullshit."

"I'm telling you."

"Isn't fart fetish just a precursor to an anal sex lover? That slippery slope that ends in a stinky hole?"

"She was."

"That's a good girl who takes it in the pooper," offered Earl.

"Oh, you meant her . . ."

Thirty minutes and a case of beer later the costume was still laid out in furry piles in the back of Earl's truck. "I can't figure out how this thing goes together," said Harry.

"Look at the directions," Earl yelled while peeing on a bush.

"They're in Chinese."

"Then look at the pictures."

"They're in Chinese, too."

***

"Why didn't we call Southern Tier Bigfoot Tours," grumbled Roy as he crawled up an incline towards the woods. Sweat poured down his face, and his shirt was drenched though he'd only traveled twenty feet. He used his hands to help propel him along, so the rifle slung on his shoulder kept slipping off and banging on the ground. He slid three feet down the incline each time he stopped to sling it over his shoulder.

"I did call. They haven't returned my phone call," said Jeff, easily walking up the incline in front of Roy.

"Then how do we know we're in the right spot?"

"This is the site of a recent sighting. The woman who claims to have hit a monkey. I believe the animal may still be in the area. At the very least, an injured animal should be easy to track. This could be the break we have been waiting for."

"So that's why we're bringing the rifles?"

"That is why we are bringing the rifles."

Deputy O'Boogie stepped out of the passenger side of the patrol car. The patrol car was parked on uneven ground along the side of the road. The car door started closing before he was completely out of the way, bumping his arm, and spilling his coffee down the front of his uniform.

"Shit."

"Whatsamatter?" asked Sheriff Paan as he placed his gold sunglasses on his face. He checked his reflection in the rear window and raised his upward lip in a lopsided sneer. Satisfied with his sneer-a-la-king, he blew his reflection a kiss.

"Nothing. This is where Mrs. Dickover believes she hit a monkey. She was heading towards town so . . ." Deputy O'Boogie nodded at the incline leading up to the woods. ". . . our monkey must have gone that way."

Sheriff Paan peered past his partner at the only other vehicle parked along the road; a late model Jeep Cherokee. "What's that sticker on the side of that Jeep?"

"It looks like a footprint."

Both men started walking towards the Jeep for a closer look.

"Sasquatch Research Organization. Who are these guys? You think they are investigating the monkey too?"

"Hmm. This investigation is getting crowded."

Peering through the back window of the Cherokee. "Sheriff, what do those cases look like to you?"

Joining the Deputy at the back of the Cherokee, Sheriff whisked off the sunglasses and leaned on the window, while framing his hands to block the glare. After a minute, the Sheriff sighed: "Those look like rifle cases."

"This is also pretty close to Ian King's projected path."

"I think the warden is gonna throw a party in the county jail[11]."

Walking back towards the patrol car. "Let's check for any clues along the side of the road, and then we'll head into the woods."

"And look for the Bigfoot hunters?"

"Mhhmm. Just curious if they've seen our missing biologist. I want to see what these boys are packing."

Patch and Harry stepped back to get the full effect. Earl, inside the Chewbacca costume, slowly turned in a circle with his arms raised like he was being arrested.

"How's it look, freaks?"

---

[11] "Jailhouse Rock", written by Jerry Leiber and Mike Stoller.

"Put your arms down, ya dork."

Earl dropped his hands to his side and fiddled with the bandoleer. He pulled a beer from the Wookie purse, inserted a straw, and maneuvered the straw between Chewbacca's lips.

"I thought something was missing. Now you look like Bigfoot."

"I'm thirsty. It's hot in here."

"No shit," Harry said as he stepping up and pinning a green ribbon to the bandoleer.

"What the hell is that?" Earl asked maneuvering his head awkwardly trying to look at his chest with the mask on.

"It's St. Patrick's Day. You need to wear something green."

"I'm not Irish."

"Doesn't matter."

"Exactly. It hasn't mattered since elementary school."

"Today it does. Today, we celebrate with our Irish brethren on their victory against sobriety by contributing to Ireland's population issue. Today, Ireland is the most populous country in the world. Being Irish is a magical place where drunkenness is totally acceptable. In fact, you can get a fine for being sober in public, and the women show their tits for plastic beads."

"Like Mardi Gras?"

"Exactly, except we don't need to be in New Orleans. There is no geographic limitations." Harry spread his arms wide. "Today. We are all Irish."

"I don't want to be Irish."

"That's because you don't know the Irish invented binge drinking."

"I want to be Irish."

"They also invented the first beer pong table. It's hidden in the Castle Jamesons-on-the-Guinness on the Isle of Pukinggreen. I heard the table is made from the gold stolen from leprechauns. The cups were dyed red from the hair of virgins. The world's first Solo cups."

"You had me at binge drinking."

"I know. Now, get out there, and act like a Bigfoot. We're going to go up to the top of that hill and look out for cars."

Patch and Harry exchanged grins as they watched Earl stumble off into the woods. In unison, they grabbed the handles of the beer cooler. They turned with the grace of synchronized swimmers, and headed up the hill. When Earl was out of earshot, Patch looked at Harry and said, "Want to smoke a bowl first? I got some new weed: Green Diesel Crippler."

Jeff stopped along the trail and turned towards Roy. He pulled a small case from his lumbar pack and carefully laid it on the ground. Flipping the plastic latches, he opened the case and turned it towards Roy. Inside lay a dozen 10 cc darts of different types.

"Here's the darts. I'll take a tranquilizer dart for the first shot. You'll have a DNA dart. For our second shots, if we get them, we'll both shoot biopsy darts. Now listen, it's very important we fire the first rounds at the same time. Nobody has ever tried to tranquilize a Bigfoot. I'm not sure on the dosage, or his reaction. The tranquilizer dart is pre-filled. It may be too weak for the individual we encounter. So, we both will need to get a clear shot. Even if we don't knock it down, we'll need the DNA dart in it too before it evades. I'm expecting the individual to not be anesthetized immediately, so we'll have to track it as it flees. Hopefully, it won't get very far. The DNA and biopsy darts both have a small light inside. The light will flash when the dart's plunger is fully depressed by firing it. This will help us find them if the darts are knocked off as it evades. The third dart is another DNA dart. I'm also giving both of us a weaker knockdown dart for emergencies. If it turns on us, and attacks, use this one, but only if there is no other option. Keep the knockdown dart separate from the other darts. We don't want to inadvertently kill the specimen."

Roy nodded along with Jeff's instructions. He was worried about encountering a real Bigfoot, and then trying to shoot it. It was one thing to rant at conferences and chat rooms about what he would do in this situation. Roy could fake machismo with the best. It was entirely different to be in the situation. He realized his posturing on how he'd handle the situation hadn't adequately prepared him to really be in the situation. Just like his first-person shooter video hadn't prepared him for combat.

Two other darts were in the case. They looked like the tranquilizer darts with a different label.

"What are those darts?"

"Those darts contain the reversal drug. We'll need to administer one to the specimen so the tranquilizer darts do not cause permanent damage."

"Wait. We have to wake it up after we dart it? We don't know how it will react. Aren't you worried it will come after us?"

"It might, but I don't need to outrun Bigfoot. I just need to outrun you," Jeff said with a wink.

Elvis may have been a country boy, but Sheriff Paan was not. He tried to be. Not much had been published on Elvis's outdoor excursions. Without historical guidance—or even one of the King's outdoor touchstones–he was left to figure it out himself. Instead, Sheriff Paan doubled his effort on copying Elvis's fashion. A bold choice that made his ineptness with anything outdoorsy more apparent. Dressing flashier than a fishing lure tended to do that. Sheriff Paan grumbled and cussed with every new snag in his sequined jumper. He thought: *Maybe I should've gone jeans and leather jacket Elvis today, or better yet, Army Elvis!* His train of thought was cut short by the sound of a white, patent leather boot sinking in mud; his white, patent leather boot.

Deputy O'Boogie also heard the sound and intervened before the sheriff could launch into a new derogatory monologue. "Who else is out here?" he asked while pointing towards a truck and a jeep parked back in the woods.

"That is Earl Stooge's truck and Patch's jeep. Harry Bear is probably with them."

Pleased with himself for changing the sheriff's mood, Deputy O'Boogie suggested they check the vehicles out.

Both officers stepped into the clearing and approached the vehicles. Tire tracks in the dirt indicated it wasn't the first time Patch, Earl, and Harry had been there. Sheriff Paan reached into the back of Earl's truck and pulled out an empty beer can, then another one, then another one. Then several more after that. "They're still cold. We must've just missed them."

Deputy O'Boogie sniffed the air. Three years before, he had his nose reconstructed to match Julian Lennon. Now he slowly rotated, angling the thin Roman schnoz into the wind. "I smell weed."

Two men in black suits moved with military

precision through the woods. Despite their dress, neither man made a sound while navigating through the underbrush. The second agent paused mid-stride and fixed his gaze three feet off the trail. Hyper alert, the first agent stopped and backtracked when his partner stopped following. Not a word was said, both agents communicated through complex hand signals. However, the final hand signal was universal. He was pointing at an 18-inch footprint. A slight smile flashed across the first agent's face before he regained his composure.

Deputy O'Boogie moved through the woods in a sine wave pattern. Like a sailboat tacking into the wind, he followed his nose toward the skunky smell. Moving back and forth across the breeze, centering on the luscious evergreen skunk epicenter.

Sheriff Paan followed him, marveling at his deputy's latest ability. *Great. Not only does he have bad taste in music, but he becomes a bloodhound in the woods.* "Smells like Martian Cotton Candy."

"It's Green Diesel Crippler," Deputy O'Boogie said with authority. He then looked nervously back at the Sheriff. "I think."

"Well, I ain't heard of that one before. Where'd you find out about it?"

"Umm, there's some in the evidence room."

"Oh yeah? I'll have to check it out. Speaking of the evidence room, those bags of weed in there seem to be getting smaller."

Deputy O'Boogie tried to look really focused by looking down in the valley to cover the guilty look on his face. "Oh really? Must be the evaporation drying out the weed. That would make the bags look smaller . . . and weigh less. A lot less."

"Yep. That's probably it."

"By the way, sheriff, I inventoried the evidence room last week and I noticed the paraphernalia from the sex party bust you did was missing."

Now it was Sheriff Paan's turn to look like he was focused on something else. "Oh, I, uh, returned that stuff. It seems the paraphernalia was just demo stuff and belonged to someone else. Like Tupperware parties."

"I see. I'll make the change to the evidence room inventory list when we get back."

Roy moved along the trail with the dart gun in the firing position, scanning side to side, in his version of how SWAT teams hold their rifles on TV shows. He moved along the trail with what he imagined was Navy SEAL precision, ready for anything. He kept his finger on the trigger guard like they do on TV. *I wish I had some face paint! I would look badass!* He looked like a fat guy playing guns.

Jeff moved casually along the trail with his dart gun hung casually on his shoulder. There was no paramilitary movie reenactment playing in his head.

"I don't know, dude. She's been different lately," Harry said as he repacked the bowl.

"Still trying to civilize you?" Patch asked, brushing the seeds and stems off the top of the cooler, and wiping his hands. He picked up the Ziploc bag full of weed, and zipped it closed. "I always knew you'd be the first to fall," he added.

"It's just, I don't know. Women are different, you know? Women see a guy, and see the potential. It's like they're buying a house. They make sure it's structurally sound, and they won't need to replace the furnace anytime soon. Then they decide to change everything about the house to suit them. They aren't satisfied with what they have. They want to improve on it. It should be like buying a car. Ya pick the model you like. The color you like. Then you live with that."

"But dudes are the ones who typically upgrade their cars with aftermarket stuff."

"Dude, I'm smoking pot. My analogies aren't working as well. Just go with me on this. Dudes want to find a great chick, and date her forever. Women find a great guy, and want to change him. I want to stay the same."

"I think they call that: 'Peter Pan Syndrome,'" Patch croaked, talking without exhaling the smoke in his lungs. He snorted as he fought his body's impulse to breathe.

"Yeah, a girl had to have coined that phrase," Harry said, suppressing a giggle. "No dude would say something like that." Harry considered the bowl a moment before raising it to his lips. "It's false advertising. A girl will be cool just long enough to hook a guy. Then she sets out to correct his faults. A guy just wants her to be the way she was when they first meet." He took another hit. "We men need to get organized. We should be able to hit them for breach of contract for changing."

"I don't know, dude. Domino is still a cool chick. She puts up with a lot."

"She is. Definitely, she is. It's just, after she got her master's and started working at the hospital, she's wanted more."

"From you?"

"Yeah."

"So, what's wrong with that?"

"Nothing. It's just she wants me to stop doing the

things I've always done and start doing the domestic-bliss thing, which I've never done. She's reinventing me without my consent."

"Like what?"

"Like, she wants me to hang out with some of her friends more, and not you and Earl so much."

"That's fucked up."

Patch's cell phone rang. A distorted ringtone from the ska-punk band Sublime echoed through the woods.

> *"I smoke two joints in time of peace*
> *and two in time of war*
> *I smoke two joints before I smoke two joints*
> *and then I smoke two more*[12]*."*

"Hey, Earl is calling," Patch choking out a cloud of smoke. He bent over coughing; handing the phone towards Harry. Harry staring the Never-Never-Land stare of a stoner at Patch's outstretched hand, bobbing his head along with the ringtone. Patch pressed the send button and answered by coughing violently into the receiver. The cell phone responded to the coughing fit with angry buzzing that sounded suspiciously like Earl cursing.

"Hey, tell him to call back. I love that song," Harry said, continuing to bob his head to the ghost of the song. He drifted away doing a white boy version of a Rastafarian dance, consisting of stomping his feet theatrically and twirling with his hands in the air. He looked like he was stomping out a fire while swatting away a fly.

Patch held the phone at his side while he wiped the tears from his eyes. "Dude! I was trying to give you

---

[12] "Smoke Two Joints", written by The Toyes.

the phone."

"I know, but I didn't want today to be 'the day the music died[13]'."

Angry buzzing continued from the cell phone.

"Dude, Earl sounds pisssssssssssssssssed." Harry giggled.

"Why's he calling on the cell phone? I mean, what the fuck?" Patch asked, glassy-eyeing Harry. He still held the cell phone at his side.

"Who the fuck knows. Maybe he's out of range of the walkie-talkie." Harry responded, glassy-eyeing Patch back.

More angry buzzing erupted from the cell phone.

"I bet that's it. I'll try the walkie-talkie to see if I can get him." Patch placed the cell phone in his cargo pants and pulled out the Fisher Price walkie-talkie. The angry buzzing became muffled, but if possible, more angry.

"Ohhhhhhhhhhhhhhhhhhh shit, dude! We forgot to put it on!" Patch said, staring intently at the knobs designed to be operated by small children. Patch's eyebrows knitted together in concentration. Harry started laughing sloppily, spraying spit everywhere. Patch looked up at him and started laughing also, surpassing Harry in phlegm distribution.

The cell phone continued to buzz angrily from Patch's pocket. The buzzing would periodically cut out as Earl's screaming rant overwhelmed the cell phone's speaker.

Both friends rolled on the ground laughing in a textbook case of stoner hysteria. Laughing consumed them, each laughing at the other one laughing until they forgot why they were laughing. Then the laughing

---

[13] "American Pie" written by Don McLean.

cycle would start again with each stick and stone poking their backs, and then the pharmaceutically-challenged attempt to stand up. Patch wiped the tears from his face again. "Aw fuck, dude. That was funny. We should tell Earl about it."

Bigfoot sniffed the air. He lifted his simian nose to the breeze. His brain sifted through the olfactory data currently being sampled, like the way we can separate one person's voice in a room full of people talking. One scent faintly rippled the surface of memory. A scented tease. He straightened his posture and took another deep, probing sniff. He catalogued the individual smells. *Deer piss, skunk piss, moose piss, someone smoking skunky cigarettes, raccoon piss, sequins, human piss, bear piss, beer; I should go find the beer, possum piss, fat guy sweating pork rinds, rabbit piss, and perfume and horse piss.* Bigfoot's heart thumped in his chest. *Perfume and horse piss? New She-Bigfoot!*

He licked his hands and ran them over his fur. He looked around him and found the closest evergreen. He marched over to the tree, snatched a handful of leaves, and stuffed them in his mouth. He chewed thoughtfully, carefully swishing the juices around his mouth. He spit the chewed leaves and chewed leaf juice into his palms, then rubbed it on his ass, balls, and face; in that order. He grimaced at the shit smell now on his hands, then reached behind him to verify the source. He sniffed his fingers again and blew out his cheeks, which is Bigfoot body language for 'something smells like shit'. He grabbed another handful of evergreen leaves and vigorously scrubbed his ass. He tossed the leaves and checked himself again. Not satisfied with the job, he backed up to the tree trunk, spread his cheeks, and wiped his ass down the trunk. He grabbed another handful of leaves and scrubbed his balls. Finally satisfied with his grooming, he strutted towards the scent of New She-Bigfoot. He grunted, purred, and clicked under his breath a Bigfoot sex-you-up song which if translated would mean: *When I'm a walking, I strut my stuff, then I'm so strung out. I'm high as a kite, I just might stop to check you out[14]*.

Sheriff Paan stopped. Earl Stooge's angry voice drifted down towards them to the left, back towards the road.

"I hear him," said Deputy O'Boogie. "Those three are probably drunk again." A safe guess considering who they were talking about. He jerked his thumb back towards the marijuana smell. "If those knuckleheads are over there, then who is smoking weed?"

"Who knows? All this aggravation ain't satisfactioning me[15]," Sheriff Paan said. He sighed to himself and rubbed his temples while he decided a plan. This monkey sighting investigation was getting more complicated than a cubic fuckload of extracurricular fuckery he could do without. He didn't want to be on this little hiking trip, and the woods already had as many ass-'tards as he typically dealt with on any Friday night at the Beaver.

"Let's find these Sasquatch Researchers," miming quotation marks with 'Sasquatch Researchers'–an irritating gesture that annoyed the shit out of Deputy O'Boogie. "Then we'll bust the potheads. Then we'll find the retard trifecta and tell them to keep it down."

"What about the monkey investigation?"

---

[14] "Blister in the Sun" written by Gordon Gano.
[15] "A Little Less Conversation" written by Mac Davis and Billy Strange.

"Fuck the monkey and the investigation. I want a drink. We'll call this circle jerk an investigation."

Deputy O'Boogie knew better than to argue when Sheriff broke from character. It was never a good sign.

Jeff paused mid-step. His foot floated momentarily before theatrically reversing. He raised his right hand to signal Roy, then braced himself to be rear-ended when he realized Roy hadn't seen the signal. Roy was still playing Navy SEAL, marveling at the hyperawareness carrying a rifle bestowed upon him. He imagined himself ninja-creeping down the corridor of some evil dictator's palace. The dictator had made a rude comment about the big, bad USA and he was dispatched to extract an apology. The A-Team theme song provided the soundtrack to the fantasy. The hyperaware, Navy SEAL, special forces, ninja of death slammed into Jeff's back. "Ow!" Roy squeaked, like all Navy SEALs do.

Jeff pushed his irritation aside. The collision had pushed him, but he had managed to avoid stepping forward. Being careful not to move his feet, he turned to Roy and pointed towards an 18-inch footprint. Roy peered around Jeff and gasped. He had never seen an actual track. He'd seen them in pictures and plaster casts, but never in real life. His gut wrenched at the thought of coming face to face with whatever made the footprint. He tucked the rifle closer to his stomach and looked worriedly around. "How old do you think the track is?"

Jeff was bent down studying the print. "Fresh. Really fresh. Look." Jeff pointed to the heel of the print. Vegetation trampled in the footprint was still springing back to their natural shape. Jeff pulled a handheld GPS from his pack and keyed in a return waypoint. Excitement welled inside him. "We'll come back to this and make a print. I don't want to lose this specimen." He checked and then rechecked the dart gun. "Let's go. We're about to make history."

Roy paused. He glanced around nervously before following. He half expected a giant troglodyte-caveman to bash his melon with a giant club any second. He hefted the dart gun up, no longer feeling much like a Navy SEAL. "How fast will the sedative work?"

Something was crashing through the woods towards Earl as he finished his piss. He pulled the costume back into place, finishing the beer before tossing the can and pulling the mask down. He crouched down behind some shrubs near an old fieldstone wall that had once been part of a long forgotten farm. He giggled to himself at the thought of scaring the shit out of Harry and Patch. The crashing sound reached a climax and abruptly stopped. He could tell they were on the other side of the fieldstone wall from by the sound of their heavy breathing. He crept toward a break in the wall. The mask obscured his peripheral vision as he swung his head around the wall ready to yell out. He jumped at the face on the other side of the wall looking back at him. Earl jerked his head back, then took a closer look. An ape was staring at him. Earl peered closer at the image while his brain tried to make sense of what he was looking at. It was nearly a reflection of his costume, but more ape-ish. An apeman. His brain rapid-fired explanations across his lobes. Earl's brain grabbed onto a likely candidate. He must be looking at a tree stump that looks weird from one angle.

Sure, happens all the time. Like when people see

animals in the clouds. It's just my brain trying to make sense of something it doesn't recognize.

Earl cocked his head to get a different perspective of the thing in front of him. Then it blinked. Earl jumped back once his brain registered that a tree stump couldn't blink. He involuntarily tried to yell "Oh, shit!", but he spazzed and stuttered. The sound coming out of his mouth sounded more like: "Oh! Sssss! Oh! Sssss! Oh! Sssss!"

The ape-man stood up. It dawned on Earl that the creature had been crouching on the other side of the wall. The thing was massive, easily eight-feet-tall. Probably 500 lbs. of ugly. It smiled at Earl, revealing a mouthful of brown and yellow canines. Earl continued his "Oh! Ssss!" mantra as he turned to run and tripped. Lying on the ground, he assumed the fetal position; protecting his face and gut from the attack he was sure to come. His mind raced while one thought popped from the chaotic stream of thoughts like a loose thread from a piece of fabric. *Did you play dead or fight an ape?* He thought he knew the answer for bears.

Damn girl! New She-Bigfoot just see Bigfoot and she start orgasm! Bigfoot like. Bigfoot always knew Bigfoot a stud. Bigfoot tell forest animal all the time. Other She-Bigfoot not know what they talk about. Bigfoot not even need to pick flower or give whiskey. New She-Bigfoot cream her pelt at the sight of Bigfoot and now she assuming mate position! Showing ass to Bigfoot because Bigfoot so sexy. Bigfoot always knew. Well, would be rude to keep New She-Bigfoot waiting. Especially when she being lady.

Patch and Harry, Sheriff Paan and Deputy O'Boogie, Jeff and Roy, and two Dark Agents all heard a scream. It wasn't exactly clear if it was a man or woman screaming. All four parties began running towards the sound. Almost. Roy dropped his rifle and began running back towards the road.

The scream sobered Patch and Harry up. They'd spent most of their lives in these woods, so they moved quickly. Years in the woods had taught them where to avoid the thick undergrowth and where the animal trails intersected.

Patch and Harry crested a small ridge and were heading down the ridge's spine when Harry noticed a fat guy running down a lower trail in the small valley on the other side. "Who the fuck is that?"

"Dunno, but he's running from something."

Harry and Patch angled down the ridge and intersected Roy's trail. They paused on the trail to watch the fat guy scramble and flail his way through the brush. Pausing to look at each other, they turned to run the opposite direction. Toward whatever the fat guy was running from.

Okay. New She-Bigfoot in sex-you-up-position like Bigfoot like. So Bigfoot smooth up behind her because Bigfoot smooth. Anyhoo, Bigfoot get on hand and knee behind New She-Bigfoot. Bigfoot make want-make-mate sound. Then sniff New She-Bigfoot. New She-Bigfoot whimper and shake with anticipation. Sexy. Anyhoo, grab New She-Bigfoot by hips and sniff ass. Real deep like Bigfoot know New She-Bigfoot will like. Then New She-Bigfoot scream! Bigfoot not know what the scream all about. That okay. Bigfoot got to take it slow. Too much for New She-Bigfoot. Maybe New She-Bigfoot erogenous zone all sensitive after make orgasm. Bet that it. Too much for New She-Bigfoot.

Jeff cursed Roy as he ran away. He picked up Roy's discarded rifle and briefly debated on wielding both weapons simultaneously. His plan hung on the two gun, two dart strategy. Jeff realized he probably couldn't shoot both rifles accurately. Carrying the second rifle would also slow him down, so he leaned Roy's rifle against a tree. He keyed in another return waypoint for the rifle. He then practiced loading and reloading his rifle quickly a few times. He'd been practicing for weeks, but he wanted to exercise the muscle memory one more time before he faced whatever lay ahead.

Jeff's entire life had been an endless series of preparations without function. His military career amounted to nothing more than practicing war with no war around. Practiced emergency procedures with no emergency coming. Eventually, he figured out that if he meticulously planned any event, from the extreme to the mundane, it would not happen. He realized this but couldn't stop it. He knew no other way. To not plan caused him anxiety of a future he wasn't prepared for. To plan negated the event. A life all dressed up with nowhere to go. *Not this time.* He headed down the trail towards history.

Earl cautiously moved from the fetal position to a crouch when he realized he wasn't going to be mauled. He remembered to keep his eyes on the ground in a submissive posture. He learned to do that from TV. Maybe it was Animal Planet. Eye contact was viewed as aggressive by something. He couldn't remember what animal he needed to avoid eye contact with or why. He was sure it was not an apeman. He'd remember that.

He'd recovered from lying on the ground waiting to be mauled. The expectation of having his inner things violently removed to become his outer things. Then the waiting for the blow. Followed by the sheepish realization claws hadn't ripped through his skin. Finally, coming to terms with the fact he was laying on the ground in the fetal position while simultaneously trying to protect his ass. He would later wonder about how quickly he had accepted his fate and assumed mauling.

The ass sniffing was not what he expected. *What the fuck was that all about?* Earl had seen dogs sniff each other's ass. Hell, he'd even had a few dogs sniff his ass. This was different. It wasn't trying to just sniff his ass. It had grabbed him, and tried to sniff his soul through his balloon knot. What had made him more uncomfortable than the sniffing was the way the creature grabbed him. It grabbed him like he was a woman. Earl felt sick with the thought. With nothing to do, his mouth busied itself by producing excess saliva and he began sweating profusely. He recognized the signs. He was about to puke. He clenched his lips and fought down the feeling. There was no way he could puke without taking off the mask. Earl shut his eyes and felt the sweat drip off his nose and pool in the inside of the Chewbacca mask's nose. At least the apeman had backed off when he screamed. Earl stretched his right leg behind him into a sprinter's starting position. He stared at the ground in front of the apeman, trying to use his peripheral vision to see the creature without pissing it off. At least not making it want to sniff his ass again.

Bigfoot crouched down in an attempt to make eye contact with New She-Bigfoot/Earl/Chewbacca. He smiled his biggest, friendliest smile. Tilting his head to orient with New She-Bigfoot/Earl/Chewbacca's, he watched as she coyly averted her eyes. He was endeared with her shyness. His fake let's-be-friends smile was replaced by a genuine smile, and he laughed out loud. He slapped the ground in front of him and hooted joyfully to himself. Hamming it up for New She-Bigfoot/Earl/Chewbacca.

Earl flinched at the ground slapping and hooting. Something about it wasn't as frightening. A universal chord was struck. The hooting seemed more like laughter than growling. Earl stole a few glances at the apeman. He was caught each time, but each glance invoked a new dance from the apeman. The dance began to take form. No longer did it resemble a freestyle dance of joy, like a dog chasing its tail for a biscuit. The dance began to include more posturing and strutting, muscle showing and strength demonstrations. Earl stood up and backed himself into the fieldstone wall. He watched the primitive dance, gradually realizing how much it resembled mating dances he'd seen in social studies class years ago. One of the few films he'd remained awake for because the native women danced topless. Big, jiggly, brown, native breasts badly in need of support. Then he noticed the apeman's crotch. There was no mistaking that.

Harry saw the rifle leaning against the tree. He didn't know what it was. Dart guns don't look like real guns. They look more like futuristic weapons. He picked the weapon up and examined it. The weight of the rifle didn't feel like a toy gun.

"See if it's loaded" Patch suggested.

Harry fiddled with the dart gun, rotating it in every conceivable direction looking for where the bullets go.

"Maybe it's a toy."

"Nah. It's too heavy to be a toy. It has an air pressure gauge. It shoots something."

"Like a paintball gun?"

"Yeah, but it doesn't have a container for paintballs. It shoots something though."

Harry held the rifle by the stock as he handed it to Patch. He felt the butt plate twist slightly. He pulled the rifle back and fully rotated the plate revealing a dart. He popped the dart free.

"What's it say?"

"DNA Specimen Dart."

"The fat guy must be a biologist? That's a nasty looking dart."

Harry mumbled his agreement and carefully replaced the dart. "I guess he didn't want DNA from whatever he's running from."

Harry handed the weapon to Patch. "Let's get Earl."

Earl pressed himself against the wall and looked around for an escape route. He resolved to get away no matter what. Nothing motivates like an ape with a boner doing a mating dance for your benefit. He watched for the apeman to turn his back while dancing. Earl pushed himself off the wall and dug his back foot into the ground for a firm purchase. He watched the apeman gyrate. *When he turns, I'm out of here.*

Bigfoot stopped dancing and cocked his head. He sniffed the air and growled softly. He focused his attention away from New She-Bigfoot/Earl/Chewbacca. Earl took the opportunity. The Apeman focused his attention in the area near Earl's escape route. Earl shifted his weight to spin on his heels. His plan was to aim for the hole in the fence to put a barrier between the horny ape and himself. He would then angle back towards the truck.

Before Earl could take a step, a hairy paw straight armed him into the stone wall. The apeman never broke his attention from the woods. He grabbed Earl's shoulder and roughly pushed him into a kneeling position. It grunted and hooted to Earl and indicated with its paw to whatever was upsetting him.

The apeman crouched and moved away from Earl. He didn't move directly towards whatever had caught his interest, but moved in an oblique path to get a better view. Earl spun and launched himself through the hole in the wall. He cleared the hole and raced up the trail. As he rounded some shrubs he felt a painful sting in his thigh. Earl pushed the pain aside and focused on his escape. The last thing he heard was the apeman roar.

Jeff was pulling the biopsy dart from the pouch when he saw the second Bigfoot. He'd waited his entire life to see, to do, something extraordinary. Now, here in these woods, was the moment he'd always waited for. The moment he'd known would come. He pushed aside the surreal feelings gripping him and focused on his task. He embraced the situation as any well-trained soldier would. Intuition guided his actions. His motions became fluid as he surrendered to instinct. Grace under pressure. He was the first person to successfully dart a Bigfoot.

The second Bigfoot rushed toward the downed Bigfoot. This one was enormous; easily three times the size of the first one. It kneeled over the first Bigfoot and gently pawed the creature. Jeff was struck by the tenderness of the touch. The touch indicated honest concern and sympathy. A touch of love. The kneeling Bigfoot looked at the dart in the smaller Bigfoot's leg, then to the human responsible. It growled. For the first time since entering the woods, Jeff felt fear. A fear that he just pissed off an enormous wild animal, and it had every right to be pissed. An odd feeling of guilt swept over Jeff. He hadn't just darted a wild animal. He did not just interrupt an animal's day, it's routine, to take some samples. His actions had caused pain and sorrow. Complex anthropomorphic emotions were shoved in his face unexpectedly. Someone could hypothesize and argue that an animal didn't have the same capability for emotions as humans understood. Jeff knew better. He'd seen them in the creature's eyes.

Jeff traded the biopsy dart for a tranquilizer dart and reloaded the rifle. Bigfoot quickly closed the gap to him and knocked the rifle out of his hands before Jeff had a chance to raise the weapon. Bigfoot's second swing knocked Jeff unconscious.

Bigfoot grabbed Jeff's shirt and roared into his face. He paused and studied Jeff. There was no reaction. Bigfoot sniffed his face. He was still breathing. Satisfied the threat was over, he dropped Jeff's body and returned to New She-Bigfoot. He looked over her for signs of life while nudging her. He leaned in close and sniffed. Bigfoot jerked his head. New She-Bigfoot was still breathing and she had beer breath.

New She-Bigfoot drink beer? Bigfoot like.

Bigfoot carefully picked up New She-Bigfoot and cradled the body to his chest. New She-Bigfoot was much lighter than he expected, like the body of a child. He held the body tighter to him. Something was crashing through the underbrush towards him. He growled softly at the new intruders and flipped New She-Bigfoot over his shoulder.

Sheriff Paan trailed behind Deputy O'Boogie

through the woods. Despite his slight, English artist frame, Winston was moving in a self-assured way over the rough terrain. Sheriff Paan had long since come to terms with the fact his outfit was beyond repair. Now he too ran swiftly, pushing himself to get ahead of his deputy.

The King doesn't come in behind nobody.

Sheriff Paan zigged low around an ancient oak as Deputy O'Boogie zagged around the other side. Coming around the other side, Sheriff Paan pulled into the lead. They broke through the underbrush onto a new trail. Directly in front of them was an old stone wall. Moving away parallel to the wall was a very large, hairy thing. Sheriff Paan didn't know what it was. He'd only caught a glimpse of the thing's face and now the thing had turned away from him. Giving him a partial view of its profile. Whatever it was, it easily tossed another creature over its shoulder and was walking upright away from him. Sheriff Paan may not be outdoorsy, but he knew enough to know when something didn't belong. He drew Elvis' .45 ACP.

Harry skidded to a halt at the sight of a man's body lying on the ground on the trail in front of him. Patch stopped at the body and checked for a pulse. Past the body, Harry could see Earl carrying something. Harry paused before calling out to Earl. Something was wrong. Whatever was in front of him was too big to be Earl. Earl would be like a child to this thing. Then Harry saw the bandolier.

Breaking from the brush between Harry and Earl, Sheriff Paan and Deputy O'Boogie stepped into view. Something glinted in Sheriff Paan's hand. Harry knew exactly what it was. Harry stepped forward and the ground under his forefoot rolled unnaturally. He looked down to see another rifle. He stared at the gun for a moment. Glancing back up, he saw Sheriff Paan hesitate. The gold pistol was pointed at the ground between the Sheriff and Earl. Then Sheriff Paan took a deep breath and pointed the barrel directly at the creature. Harry picked up the discarded dart gun and aimed it at the sheriff and pulled the trigger. The rifle kicked slightly with a compressed air thump.

Deputy O'Boogie hesitated drawing his own weapon. He rested his hand on the pistol on his hip. He knew he should draw his weapon with the sheriff, but he didn't know enough about the situation to introduce firearms. He was still considering his options when Sheriff Paan threw his shoulders back and fell forward. A small cylinder stuck out of his back.

What the hell is that?

Harry was still holding the dart gun when Deputy O'Boogie saw him. Harry realized he was shaking as he dropped the rifle and raised his hands. "Whoops."

23

"Dance Like a Monkey"
~New York Dolls

The cinderblock caved in from the blow. The tallest Dark Agent pulled his hand free and studied the softball size hole in the wall. He brushed the dust from his suit and adjusted his cuffs. His sneer deepened into a canyon etched with malice. No blood, no boxer's fracture, no scrapped skin, no redness and swelling; his knuckles were free of the usual signs of solid object punching.

In one swift movement, he spun on the agent who delivered the report. The baton slipped from the wrist holster into his hand and centrifugal force locked the form-fitting metal cylinders into place. The blow shattered the agent's skull above the ear. The agent dropped without uttering a cry. The dropped bowling ball sound of the assault hung in the air.

The tallest Dark Agent moved to the remaining agent. He casually unbuttoned the agent's suit jacket and wiped the baton on the agent's tie. The agent stood at attention, eyes straight forward. There is a story told by people excessively concerned with people standing without fidgeting to recruits in boot camp. The general theme of the story is the Queen of England allowed herself to be stung by a bee rather than move, and therefore disgrace herself, during the country's national anthem. The agent's bearing would have made the Queen Mother proud.

The tallest Dark Agent casually returned the steel

baton. His moves were well practiced. Absent were the fumbling one might associate with attaching a weighted steel cylinder to a wrist holster. His movements were as sure as someone putting on a watch. "Now. Tell me the story again." Moving himself to look directly in the agent's eyes, "Ensure you clarify how you allowed the target to escape. Include how another *gigantopithecus*[16] in this sector escaped your knowledge. Please, do not leave out any detail. You will not be able to tell the story again when you are finished. Is that clear?"

The agent completed his report exactly as the pile of meat previously known as his partner had done. The report was heavy with details, void of unsubstantial observations. The agent did not offer to speculate on the additional Bigfoot or the escape.

The operational directive for Dark Agents was strictly clandestine. All contact was exclusively at their choosing and discretion. More than a strategic principle, this tenet was the keystone of their society. Guarding secrets was far easier if you didn't advertise you possessed them. They were even easier to guard if no one knew you existed.

The rules of engagement had been loosened for this mission. The objective was to eliminate the rouge Bigfoot, but not at the expense of operational secrecy. An engagement with six human civilian witnesses, six civilians who would need eliminating, provided an equally unsatisfactory outcome. Operationally, it was better to maintain covert observations and engage at a more suitable time. Either way, the agent was going to

---

[16] In 1985, Professor Grover Krantz tried to formally name Bigfoot by presenting a paper at the meeting of the International Society of Cryptozoology, assigning it the binomen *Gigantopithecus blacki*.

be standing in this very same spot, with the very same results. It was easy for the agent to accept his fate knowing all paths would have led him and his partner to the same outcome.

The agent completed the report. Leaving no operational stone unturned. He turned with a brisk military move. He then stepped forward to a grey locker on the wall and entered the combination on the keypad. He opened the locker door, turning to face the inside door. An assortment of small edged weapons of different styles were mounted on the door. The weapons were designed for close quarter battle, hand-to-hand combat in tight spaces. They were the most personal of weapons. The agent selected a KA-BAR Tanto. The knife looked very similar to a miniature Samurai's sword. The agent returned to his place and kneeled on the floor, leaning back to sit on his feet. Seppuku, the Japanese suicide ritual, involves the suicidee sticking a small ceremonial sword into his belly and slicing, from left to right, spilling all his stuffing on the floor. Whoever said suicide was painless never saw this method.

The agent followed the seppuku ritual by detailing his dishonor in fluent Japanese.

"Don't bother" the tallest Dark Agent interrupted, drawing an ancient flintlock pistol from his shoulder holster, and pointing it at the agent. The agent adjusted his grip on the knife. He was determined to do the job himself. It was his first and only opportunity for a "fuck you" to his soon-to-be-former boss. The classic *you can't fire me because I quit.*

Sensing the agent's intentions, the tallest Dark Agent interrupted again. "Do you know why I still carry this old flintlock?"

He moved the weapon so the agent could examine

the pistol's profile. Both the agent's and tallest Dark Agent's eyes fell to the weapon. One set of eyes looked at the pistol fondly; a treasured keepsake. The other, out of shock. In his long tenure with the Dark Agency, his boss had never spoken to him with any candor. Over half a century of employment had not illuminated one facet of the man beneath the mask. The other reason the agent listened was simple greed. He had once been human. Even though his humanity was long gone, the residue of his former nature remained. Like a sweater hung on a hanger, his psyche retained the shape of his past. His humanity bubbled to the surface in this moment. Now, he wanted, needed, to hear a human voice. After decades of the only conversation he ever participated in was sanitized, institutional, and operational; any intimacy was comforting. Even if the connection was with a despicable monster. Whatever the monster revealed about its true nature would be something similar to closure, and it would have to do.

"It is bulky and filthy when fired. Black smoke and powder residue get into everything. It's the wood. The polymer injected molding of today's weapons lack the life of organic material. It's heavy. The weight makes me pay attention. It puts me in the moment. Other pistols feel like toys compared to the heft of an old flintlock. The sound of the action is unmistakable. The metallic sound of the hammer being pulled back just sounds . . . like a gun to me. I've always enjoyed the sound. I think many people do. Have you ever watched a movie? I am referring to a movie where a character draws a gun. In the movie, the gun always makes a cocking sound when drawn, regardless of the type of gun. Yet we both know a double-action semiautomatic pistol makes no such sound when drawn. One would be foolish to fire a weapon that rattled like that. I believe it's because there's a primal reaction to the sound. The tone resonates with the listener. This flintlock makes that sound, and I find it pleasing to my ear."

The tallest Dark Agent continued, "It was my first pistol. The firearm offered detachment. It had been all swords and maces, spears and axes before then. Intimate weapons which required exhausting fights. The blood and sweat always ruined my clothes. Not my blood or sweat, of course, but blood doesn't have enough courtesy not to splatter someone else's clothing. I've always found that curious. Blood is the nectar of life. It carries the essential elements to maintain an organism's life. It is similar to saltwater in purpose and chemical make-up. The same saltwater where life first sprang. Yet it has no conscience." Turning the pistol back to the agent, "The weight is a gift."

The door opened before the echo finished reverberating off the walls. Four agents entered the room with identical movements, like synchronized swimmers in business suits. The first and third agents removed the two bodies. The second and fourth agents stood at attention directly in front of the tallest Dark Agent, who coolly wiped an eighteenth century flintlock with a black handkerchief. The two new agents were identical to the two corpses being carried out of the room.

The tallest Dark Agent regarded the two new agents before speaking. "I do not want to have this conversation again . . ."

24

"Blue Collar Suicide"
~The Refreshments

"Mangrove, what the hell is this?" Echo demanded, waving a piece of paper in his face.

Mangrove was a conflict-avoiding weasel. He knew Echo wouldn't be happy with the piece. She'd been pushing for 'real news' pieces for months.

What was real news now? I'll tell you what is: whatever the network says it is. Networks are corporations with trustees and shareholders, sponsors and campaign contributions. I have news for you, honey. The news are those beautiful numbers on the shareholder's checks. We make the news that make those numbers get bigger, and we don't report the news that makes those numbers get smaller. That is accomplished by a delicate balance of skewing the news to agree with our core demographic's belief system. It makes them feel safe, it makes them feel smarter because their news coincides with their sensibilities. We allow the viewers to say, "I told you so" on a nightly basis.

Then, you know what happens? You want to know what those self-righteous, loyal viewers whose egos just got a digital hand job a la our newscast? They go shopping! And what do they buy? The products advertised on our show! Why? Because we just reassured them they were smart and they were right. We tell them to consume every night, and they do. Like a horny teen with octopus arms rounding first base in the backseat. *They grab and grope at whatever we tell them to. How else do you think we get them to still buy those crappy American car models? Because we run magnified negative reports on the better foreign cars! Do you think anyone would shop in a store that sells clothing made in sweatshops? No? Well, we run Old Navy ads during our newscasts. Want to know what happens? Online sales go up 6.5 percent. Want to know what they buy? Apparel silkscreened with American flags that were made in Sri Lanka. Because it isn't that it was not made in the U.S.A., or that it has Old Glory printed on it; it's because we told them to consume it. Never mind the clothes are so cheap because we don't want to pay an American to make the same shirt, even if there are a lot of Americans out there who could really use a job.*

We create the self-licking ice cream cone. The news shapes their belief systems, then we report the news which supports said manufactured beliefs. When we need them to be docile and obedient, we run news that strums that chord. When we need them to rally against an issue, we pull that wire. We tell them what the core issues are and when they matter. Ever notice you only hear about Social Security and abortion during an election? We wind those issues up and attach easily digestible polling data to each candidate. Those same issues become part of each candidate's platform. But nothing ever comes of it. Did you know, George Bush senior pushed the abortion issue in the '80s? We conduct digital psychological warfare and put big oil back in the White House. For 20 years, we've strummed the same song with every election, with the promise that this time it will be resolved. We've pulled that stunt for 20 years, and we'll pull it for another 20 years.

Remember the spotted owl? Tree huggers and consumers battling for the life of a nocturnal bird most people will never see? That was us. Do you know how many acres of forest there are in the continental United States? The forest industry could have easily selected another site; left the owl alone. But you know who one of our shareholders is? The timber industry. They came to us with a small problem, and we gave them a solution by winding up our viewers. And guess who's a shareholder for life?

We are the tail that wags the dog, the opium of the masses, the something-up-the-sleeve, and the hand that distracts you from the trick. Nightly, we make the Kool-Aid, and we make it taste any way our viewers want.

That's what Mangrove Slimebucket would have *liked* to say to Echo. There was no way he was really going to *say* that. Not to Echo. She was beautiful and intense. She wouldn't be cowed by Mangrove's verbal diarrhea. And she was a woman. Mangrove didn't do well convincing women, except convincing them his last name suited him; like a pastry chef with the last name of Baker. Mangrove was a coward.

"What? It's a good piece."

"A Bigfoot sighting? Are you fucking kidding me? Send it to one of those science fiction channels so they can dramatically recreate it. This . . ." she said, punctuating each syllable by jabbing the paper in his face, " . . . is not news. What about my piece on the county waste treatment plant dumping raw sewage in the river? We already taped a Bigfoot piece when something harassed those campers, and you didn't even show it. Why would we do another one?" She crossed he arms and flexed her toned muscles, physically dominating her station manager.

"That's the piece you're doing. Get over to Mrs.

Dicklover's with a camera crew and film something."

"You're Freudian slipping, it's 'Dickover.'" Echo stomped away back to her office. *Maybe there was something to these Bigfoot sightings. Two in a month? I'll check to see what the Sheriff has.*

25

"Bury My Heart at the Trailer Park"
~Roger Clyne and the Peacemakers

Earl's mind slowly ascended from the tranquilizer depths. Awareness wasn't bringing anything he was interested in. Memory fragments broke the surface but the puzzle pieces did not make sense. What he was sure of was he was having the worst hangover of his life, and Earl was familiar with hangovers. It would be easier to list the times he didn't wake up with one. This one was brutal. His head pounded with every pump of his heart. Like each platelet of blood was issued tiny baseball bats and were busy beating the shit out of his brain in hydrodynamic-coordinated attacks. His throat hurt from breathing through his mouth. Then there was the troubling feeling he'd pissed himself. Between the pounding of the blood pressure drumbeat assaulting his melon, an uneasy feeling scratched at the pit of his stomach. *I had the weirdest dream last night.* Chemically induced amnesia begets confusion begets anxiety begets dread.

Earl opened his eyes, which took some effort. He couldn't remember ever being so hungover that he couldn't open his eyes. Eyes are the fly in a hangover's ointment. The excited kids up way too early for cartoons. Plenty of times he didn't want to open his eyes, but never with real difficulty. Opening eyes shouldn't be difficult. Infants seconds out of the womb can do it. The feature kind of comes with the lids.

It was dark outside. He still had the mask on. Peering through the mask's eye holes rocked his memory back. Earl would've jerked if he could have moved.

Oh, shit. Oh, shit. Oh, shit. That wasn't a dream. The Icarus moment when you've realized you've screwed yourself in a completely new and novel way.

He remembered climbing a tree when he was a little boy and falling out of it. The fall had knocked his wind out. Now he was having the same helpless, panicky feeling. He tried to move but his limbs wouldn't respond. He tried to concentrate on moving his fingers, but how? How do you focus your will to move muscle groups when you've never needed to do it before? He tried to imagine his finger moving and project the idea to his finger. Like the muscles just needed a power-point brief to remind them what they were supposed to be doing. He thought of a Metallica song about being trapped inside a body that couldn't move. He couldn't remember what the song was about. Something to do with soldier with a venereal disease. The smell of sweat and piss wafted from the inside of the Chewbacca costume and escaped through the holes in the face mask. The parade of truck-stop bathroom odors was making him nauseous.

Earl's stomach dropped. Something was moving outside of his field of view. He knew immediately it was the apeman. The sound of vegetation moving and then being laid down next to him. He concentrated on the sounds around him, trying to figure out where he was. Trying to get some mental picture of what was happening. High above him, he watched the blinking lights of an airplane flying miles above his head. A plane full of happy people flying somewhere exciting.

A plane full of people who weren't being held hostage by a horny apeman. Earl opened his mouth to scream but only dry, scratchy sounds escaped. The horny-apeman-rustling-through-the-bushes sounds stopped.

I probably shouldn't have done that.

26

"Last to Know"
~Alejandro Escovedo

Deputy O'Boogie turned from Harry to the sheriff, staring in disbelief. He kneeled down and checked for the sheriff's pulse. Satisfied with the result, he yanked the dart out of him and stuffed it into an empty compartment on his belt. Patch had moved next to Harry, Winston drew his Glock on both of them. He had never drawn his weapon in his tenure on the force. Now adrenaline coursed through his body. He felt like a sheriff's deputy for the first time in his life. He and the sheriff had their differences. In fact, they didn't agree on anything. It didn't help the sheriff's supposed biological father hated John Lennon; the father of Deputy Winston O'Boogie's chosen idol. Despite the differences, they were partners, and although neither would admit it, they were friends. Elvis would never be Deputy Winston O'Boogie's king, and he never believed he was the King of Rock and Roll. Elvis was a rocker, so even if they didn't belong to the same church, the shared the same religion. Winston was not aware of his feelings for the sheriff until now. He also didn't want the retard trifecta to shoot him too.

"Freeze, mother fucker!"

"Whoa, Winston. Is that a Julian Lennon song?" Harry asked.

"No and shut the fuck up!" Deputy O'Boogie yelled, scratching his voice. Winston could sing Julian Lennon pitch-perfect. The Julian Lennon catalogue didn't include any screaming, so Winston's voice wasn't accustomed to yelling. The sound seemed strange to him; adding to the surrealism of the situation.

"Oh. Well, why are you yelling, dude?"

"Yeah. Why are you yelling, dude?" Patch echoed, still holding the other dart gun.

Deputy O'Boogie noticed the dart gun in Patch's hand and stepped back into a defensive stance. "Drop your weapon!"

"Winston, cut your shit. Earl's gone," Harry said as he smacked the dart gun out of Patch's hand.

"You are under arrest. You have the right to remain silent . . . and . . . go fuck yourself, and . . . ride in the backseat of the patrol car, and . . . eat jail food without bitching, and . . . buy tickets for the Annual Sheriff's Ball, and . . .," Deputy O'Boogie stammered as he felt around for the Miranda Rights cheat sheet he kept in his belt. Without his notes, the only parts of the declaration he remembered was whatever was said in the movies. Not finding his notes, he ad-libbed: " . . . and you are hereby bound by law to tell me what the fuck you did to the sheriff . . . and to help me carry him out of the woods . . . "

"Wow, Winston, you sound like a real pig!" Patch said, nodding his head appreciatively.

"Yeah, I've never heard you do pig-talk before. You could be on *Cops*. Both Patch and Harry slacker-slouched; not raising their hands or acting even remotely like they were being arrested. Both ignored the 9 mm pistol pointed at them.

Deputy O'Boogie then added: "And you are hereby commanded to dump that weed, and not to tell the Sheriff you got it from me."

"What about the sex toys I got from sheriff?"

"You can keep them."

Moaning from behind Harry and Patch interrupted the arrest. Deputy O'Boogie, Harry, and Patch all turned towards the sound. Only Jeff's head was in view.

"Who the fuck is that?" asked Deputy O'Boogie, flicking the joint they'd been smoking over his shoulder.

"Dunno. We found him lying on the trail," Patch said.

Deputy O'Boogie adjusted his uniform and tried to regain his composure. He closed his eyes and counted to ten; said a quick prayer to Marley and Mary Jane, the patron saints of potheads to not let him look too stoned. He started down the trail towards the moaner while trying to project some sort of authority figure vibe. "Sir, this is Deputy O'Boogie. Are you in need of assistance?"

Jeff sat up and held his head in his hands. His jaw ached and he tasted blood. His right ear was ringing. He stood up shakily and rubbed his jaw. The left side of his jaw hurt where it attached to his skull.

It must have hit me on the right side of the head, knocked my jaw, and hyper-stressed the tendons.

Jeff busied himself by poking his tragus, the little flap of skin in front of the ear, trying to stop the ringing when he noticed a sheriff's deputy in front of him.

Roy was hopelessly lost. He'd stumbled, tripped, flopped, and blundered along the trail. He'd been too busy super-ninja fantasizing to notice which way Jeff had led them into the woods. Now he crashed back and forth along the valley trail that paralleled the highway. On the other side of the ridge was his car. He was never going to find it if he remained in the valley.

After leaving Jeff, guilt gripped Roy, and he turned back to help his friend. Roy played different scenarios in his head.

Maybe Jeff had solved the situation, and I could still share some of the credit. Maybe Bigfoot killed Jeff. Then I could recover the body. Write a book. Become famous. Then no one would know I was a coward.

Then the guilt took over the driver's seat.

Jeff is my friend and I just left him out there with that thing.

Soon, wishful thinking had to throw it's two cents in.

Well, Jeff was in the military. He knows what to do. He probably escaped.

Next in line was blame-storming.

I wasn't in the military, goddammit! I'm not trained to deal with those kind of situations. Jeff should have trained me, or at least warned me about what it was going to be like.

Roy stopped in the middle of the trail, and stared at the ground. He needed to go back. He turned around for the dozenth time, and headed the wrong way down the trail.

Besides, Jeff has the GPS to get me the hell out of these godforsaken woods.

Deputy O'Boogie managed to herd Jeff, Patch, and Harry over to the sheriff. Jeff and Harry looked at each other sheepishly, exchanging self-conscience smiles and abbreviated eye rolls. Patch space-cadet stared at nothing with a lopsided, stoner smile on his face. Deputy O'Boogie exhausted the extent of his emergency first aid and how-to-wake-passed-out-people knowledge. "What the hell was in the dart?"

"An animal tranquilizer. The dosage was for a much larger animal. I can give him a reversal dart which should neutralize the tranquilizer dart," Jeff said.

"Do it."

Jeff pulled out a pouch and removed a dart with the reversal drug.

Deputy O'Boogie looked at the dart. It looked like a mean hybrid between a hypodermic needle and a throwing dart. "I'll do it. What do I do?"

"You just stab him with it."

Deputy O'Boogie kneeled, and poked the dart needle into the Sheriff's ass cheek. The small observation window on the side of the dart indicated the reversal drug wasn't going into the sheriff. "Why isn't it working?"

"The dart is designed to be fired from a gun. Maybe you have to hit him harder with the dart." Jeff speculated.

Deputy O'Boogie removed the dart, and slammed down on the sheriff's ass. The dart window indicated no change. Winston, getting frustrated, grabbed the dart and repeated with more force. The dart window remained full. The deputy grabbed the dart and double-fist slammed the dart into the sheriff's ass cheek. The sheriff's body bowed from the blow, flopping into a new discarded rag doll pose. The dart remained full. Winston sat back, then repeatedly slammed the dart into the sheriff's ass cheek. He looked like a monkey having a seizure while trying to tenderize a piece of meat with a sewing needle. After the last blow, he sat back and watched for any changes in the observation window. He groaned when the only result of his tantrum was bubbles in the reversal drug. Red dots began appearing all over the seat of the sheriff's pants. Patch started giggling. "Hey, he's spotting!"

Harry reached for the dart, "Let me try." Harry kneeled over the sheriff's other cheek. "I read you need to aim three inches below the surface of what you are hitting." He held the dart over his head with his right hand, closed his eyes in a stoner approximation of a Zen meditation, and slammed the dart down. The sheriff's body jumped from the blow. They all kneeled down to look at the dart's window. No change. Harry snatched the dart and began pounding it into the sheriff's ass. He ended with a new technique: holding the dart like a nail and hammering it with the palm of his hand.

"Maybe it needs to be fired from the gun?" Jeff suggested loading the rifle. Everyone stepped back as Jeff aimed the dart gun at the sheriff. "I only have one dart. Maybe we should set him up in a better position."

Winston and Harry dragged the sheriff to a fallen log and flopped his body over it. They arranged him to maximize ass exposure. Blood dots were growing and merging on the back of the Sheriff's pants.

Jeff stepped back and fired.

The Sheriff jumped up from the log and looked at the party behind him. "Why does my ass hurt?"

27

"Rebel Without a Clue"
~Tom Petty and the Heartbreakers

Bigfoot worried about New She-Bigfoot. She no move since being shot. Carry to Bigfoot den. Give her Bigfoot bed. Make new bed for Bigfoot. Because Bigfoot gentleman. Make two separate beds. No want to crowd New She-Bigfoot. Leaves of beds touching. Like beds' hands grazing each other. That good enough for Bigfoot now. Bigfoot not want be creepy. Like squirrel. Human not know but squirrel big perv. Always try sneak in Bigfoot bed. Say Bigfoot warm but Bigfoot know better. Offer Bigfoot back rub, but back rub always go lower and lower. Bigfoot not stupid. Little, rodent, nut-cracking fingernails scratching Bigfoot sensitive skin. Feel like getting licked by cat. Bigfoot no let cat lick anymore. One cat want groom Bigfoot all day. Not so bad. Bigfoot look nice, but smell bad. Cat breath smell like cat lick fish asshole.

Bigfoot have issue with dating so really hope New She-Bigfoot okay. Try dating service: Ehairy.com. Try to find She-Bigfoot want make mate. Seem like good idea. Before, Bigfoot try meet She-Bigfoot in woods. Bigfoot never know how She-Bigfoot going to be. Bigfoot need to get She-Bigfoot attention. Throw rocks at She-Bigfoot. Kiss rocks first to let She-Bigfoot know interested. So, try dating service. Like ordering from menu. Tell what Bigfoot want in She-Bigfoot:

Want mate.
No talk.

Get food.

No talk.

No want improve Bigfoot.

No talk.

In that order. No big deal. What Bigfoot get? She-Bigfoot want talk, talk, talk. Want talk before mate. Bigfoot no want talk so no make big mate. She-Bigfoot say need get to know Bigfoot. Bigfoot show She-Bigfoot his Captain Kielbasa. She-Bigfoot say inappropriate. Bigfoot say this all She-Bigfoot need to know about Bigfoot before mate. Now Bigfoot kicked off Ehairy.com. Not return Bigfoot money. Ehairy.com say guarantee Bigfoot mate. Bigfoot not care with who. Just want She-Bigfoot come and make mate. No talk, make mate, then go. Want Ehairy.com send new She-Bigfoot for mate. Now Ehairy.com block Bigfoot. Say not sex service. Then what the purpose? Bigfoot send money, Ehairy.com find mate, Bigfoot make big mate, Ehairy.com find new mate; rinse, repeat. Not see problem.

Anyhoo. Bigfoot worried. Smelled Dark Agents in woods. They must be after New She-Bigfoot. Dark Agents bad. Create problem for Bigfoot. If Bigfoot break twig and human find it; Dark Agents come. Bigfoot seen; Dark Agents come. Bigfoot heard; Dark Agents come. Now Bigfoot need to dig hole for poop. Bigfoot here before human, now Bigfoot need to hide poop. Human have poop fetish and it Bigfoot problem. Why not tell human no play with Bigfoot poop? Bigfoot know why. Dark Agents speciest. Not care about Bigfoot quality of life. Bigfoot oppressed by the man.

Dark Agents say Bigfoot going to be naturalized. No more hiding. Bigfoot can live in peace in woods. Bigfoot live in peace in woods now. Only thing come bug Bigfoot is human. Think bullshit. Bigfoot not need naturalization. Bigfoot need make mate and refund from Ehairy.com.

Think Dark Agents after New She-Bigfoot. New She-Bigfoot must be rebel. Don't worry, New She-Bigfoot. Bigfoot hide you, my hairy, rebel angel. Poor, crazy, mixed up New She-Bigfoot. Viva, New She-Bigfoot. Live on the run with New She-Bigfoot.

So Bigfoot outlaw now. Feels good. Bigfoot always want to be outlaw. Bigfoot not like any rule, so not do rule. She-Bigfoot say that mean Bigfoot antisocial and lazy, not outlaw. Outlaw need to have focus. Be outlaw one thing. Like Robin Hood. Steal from rich and give to poor. That okay because poor like get money. Only insult rich. Bigfoot insult everyone. Not care. So She-Bigfoot say Bigfoot just asshole. Bigfoot piss on She-Bigfoot den. Say: How that for outlaw? She-Bigfoot throw rock at Bigfoot. No kiss first. Bigfoot not see why so mad. Bigfoot one time pay good money to get piss on. Not so bad. So, New She-Bigfoot going show Bigfoot how be outlaw.

Oh. Bigfoot think hear New She-Bigfoot.

28

My Shit's Fucked Up
~Warren Zevon

Jeff paced his jail cell. The cell door was wide open, but he had not recrossed the threshold once he had entered it. He washed his hands to remove the remaining ink from being fingerprinted. Jeff had never been arrested, and the news was not sitting well with him. A lifetime of law-abiding behavior erased with this one arrest. Jeff imagined his reputation tarnished. Yet, in the back of his head, he realized what outlaws found out long ago. Nobody cared about your good behavior. It was expected, there was no pat on the back coming. Bad behavior got people's attention. It was why cartoons of bad kids were far more popular than cartoons of good kids; the *Calvin and Hobbes* syndrome.

What until the boys at the VFW hear about this one.

Patch and Harry were standing in the hall separating the cells talking to Deputy O'Boogie. "Winston, we've got to go back to the woods. Something has Earl."

"Harry, the joke has gone too far. You darted the sheriff. You three really screwed the pooch this time."

"We aren't joking this time. That hairy thing grabbed Earl. He's still out there."

"You aren't going anywhere until the sheriff is back from the hospital."

"We don't have that long. That thing was carrying

141

Earl off over its shoulder. It could be eating Earl right now."

"Anything that ate Earl would just get drunk and gassy. Are you guys being serious? You don't know what has Earl? No dicking around this time, either."

Harry grabbed Winston by both shoulders, looked into his eyes, "I don't know what grabbed Earl."

"I do," Jeff as he stepped into the hall.

"What? Bigfoot?" asked Harry.

"Yes. That is exactly what I think. My question for you is: why was your friend dressed up as Bigfoot?"

Harry and Patch exchanged looks. Reading each other's minds, as if their synapses were catapulting information across the void to the other's brain. With conspicuous nods, they both determined it was time to come clean.

Patch sighed, "We've been hoaxing Bigfoot." After saying it, the floodgates in Patch's brain opened, his mouth spewing faster than his mind could keep up. "We started a Bigfoot tour company and were charging people to take them out where the sightings were."

"You've been doing what? You've been hoaxing Bigfoot?" Jeff inflating with self-righteous dogma, "I've been fighting people like you my entire career as a researcher. Do you know how much work you cause us? How much damage hoaxers do to our credibility? The Sasquatch Research Organization has been trying to reveal the truth about Bigfoot. To try to inform the public about the creature's existence . . . Every time a real sighting is investigated and made public, some hoaxer comes out of the woodwork claiming responsibility! What does media focus on? The hoax! Even if the evidence is real, all of the hoaxes are replayed on the news, refreshing the public's memories. We have reputable scientists, highly-qualified field researchers, some very serious evidence, yet we cannot be taken seriously because of people like you. And to make money at it? You are scam-artists. Deputy, arrest these men!" Jeff said, both feet planted firmly on his chosen soapbox.

"Whoa, whoa. We can't be arrested. We're already under arrest," Harry said. "We've been getting paid by some guys to do this."

"Who would pay you to scam people?" asked Jeff.

"Dunno, some guys in suits. They were feds or from the state. They pay us to keep posting hoaxes on our website, and selling tours."

"Did these men know you were dressing as Bigfoot?" asked Jeff.

"Uh, nope. I don't think so. We were still hoaxing evidence back then: footprints, hair samples, Bigfoot poop. We hadn't moved into dressing up then."

"You make Bigfoot poop?"

"Yeah! Want to know how?"

"No!" Jeff and Winston said in unison.

Deputy Winston O'Boogie scanned the faces of his three prisoners, recovering from the shock of what he was hearing. "Well, according to you, a Bigfoot is in the area." Winston looked directly into Jeff's eyes. He was not in the mood to go down this road. "Either you convince me Bigfoot exists and grabbed Earl, or . . ." Winston paused for effect, letting the silence hang. ". . . you tell me Bigfoot doesn't exist, and they've been scamming innocent people. You don't get both."

Jeff recognized the *Catch 22* logic play immediately. He followed the thread one step further and realized if he pushed for justice, the way the cards were laid out with Deputy O'Boogie, he would be denouncing his own research and the SRO. Then he could be guilty of the same crime committed by the hoaxers. The SRO requested donations from amateur hunters, charged membership fees, and charged Bigfoot enthusiasts for camping trips into areas where bigfoot sightings had been investigated by the SRO. Not to mention they'd lose the few research grants the organization was able to get. If the SRO found out he implied Bigfoot did not exist, he would lose his credentials, and he'd be fired.

He also realized he was going to have a tough time going after a couple of locals in a small town. Jeff was from a small town, so he understood the loyalty a tight-knit community fostered. Outsiders were accepted but never fully assimilated into the community. His credibility would be even more suspect because of his chosen profession. No, he should wait to play this card later. There was a Bigfoot out there. He'd seen it. Hell, it nearly knocked his head off. He could push for justice after he gets proof of its existence. Then he could go after these hoaxers. The deputy would have a harder time pushing the *Catch 22* then. "Your friend has been captured by a Bigfoot."

"What would a Bigfoot want with Earl?" asked Winston. "How did it get Earl anyway?"

"I think I may have darted your friend. My partner and I were investigating a sighting in the woods when we heard a terrible scream. My partner, Roy, lost his nerve and ran back down the way we came. I pressed on towards the sound. I came upon an old fieldstone wall out in the woods. A small Bigfoot ran out onto the trail. I fired my dart gun, hitting it in the thigh. That's when a second Bigfoot came out. A much bigger one; a size more typical of reports of the species. While I reloaded the dart gun, the second creature knocked me out. Now, after hearing what you three have been up to; I think the smaller Bigfoot I darted was your friend."

Jeff shifted his eyes from the ground to Patch and Harry. "I think the larger Bigfoot believes your friend is another of his kind."

"You darted Earl?" Harry asked.

"I believe so. It wasn't my intention to, but in my defense, he was dressed as a Bigfoot."

Winston looked up at the ceiling, trying to take it all in. "How did you get a Bigfoot costume, anyway?"

"Not Bigfoot; Chewbacca," Patch said proudly, adjusting his eye patch. "I noticed how similar Chewbacca was to the photos of Bigfoot one night, and I mentioned it to Harry. It kinda grew out of that."

"We thought it was a safe idea. We figured we could make a little money. What would be the harm?" added Harry. "We've worked on different ways to hoax Bigfoot, then when word of mouth built up enough steam, we launched the tour company." He looked at Jeff apologetically, "We didn't think we were hurting anyone. Bigfoot didn't exist, right?"

"Okay," Winston said. "I'm having some trouble getting my head around this. You . . ." pointing at Jeff, " . . . say Bigfoot exists." Shifting to Patch and Harry, "You two have been dressing up like Bigfoot to sell tours. Here's the part that gets sticky." Switching back to Jeff, "You think a Bigfoot mistook Earl for another Bigfoot. Why? I mean, wouldn't it know the difference? How dumb are these things?"

"Umm, that I can't say. Bigfoot is believed to be solitary creatures. Perhaps it doesn't interact with much with others of its kind. Maybe it isn't self-aware enough, at least not to the point where it would notice the differences between itself and a human in a Chewbacca suit.

"As far as intelligence, we believe the creatures are very intelligent. They've managed to avoid human populations for this long. However, this scenario may not be an indication of intelligence. The creature may never have experienced this sort of masquerade. It doesn't have a concept of something in a costume. This falls outside its knowledge. Something like when deer run out in front of cars. Deer only understand the speed of the natural world, the speed they or a fox can move. A car moving at 70 mph is just off the charts. They can't conceive of it, so they judge distances based on velocities they understand."

"Well, we know where that gets them. What happens if this Bigfoot figures out Earl is not a Bigfoot?"

"We need to get to him before that happens."

29

"Big Brown Eyes"
~Old 97's

Echo dragged her cameraman towards the sheriff's station. "Roger, get your ass over here."

Roger quickly shook his head, pointed back to the news van.

"We talked about this. Don't you have a journalistic bone in your body?"

"How is breaking-and-entering equal to journalism on your planet?"

"I have a hunch."

"I have a hunch too. The station is going to be reporting on the scandalous incarceration of their investigative reporter and her cameraman. Aren't you supposed to be on vacation after your attack?"

"What attack? Two guys broke into my loft under suspicious circumstances. I wasn't attacked. They were. If you don't help me, I'll tell your wife about the time you touched my tit."

"That was an accident! I was reaching for the camera!"

"Doesn't matter. Women don't care about those things. They only care about their husbands and handfuls of other women's flesh."

"I'll just suffer the consequences. It was an accident. I've got nothing to hide."

"I'll show her the video we did at the lake. The one where you couldn't keep the camera on me, and kept filming the girls in bikinis. Talk your way out of that one, Gandhi."

"You wouldn't."

"I think we both know I would."

"Okay, but tell me the truth. Why are we breaking into the station? Why can't we just ask the sheriff for whatever we need?"

"Remember the piece we did on the campers getting raided by Bigfoot?"

"Yeah?"

"I tried to pull it up for a reference before we went out to investigate the sighting. It's gone."

"So? It was a crap story. Someone probably just deleted it."

"No. We *never* delete a story. We hold onto everything. How else could we zing a candidate for waffling on a subject if we deleted everything? It's not even the station's policy. It comes from the parent company. At the very least, we always keep the reels. The reel is gone too. The logs are also missing. That reel never existed. The logs say we didn't check out any reels that day. My notebook entries are gone. I looked at your notes, they're gone, too."

"Maybe you missed it."

"No. I looked everywhere. I couldn't trace any of the files. Then I looked at the editing computer. The hard drive had been slicked."

"How do you know?"

"I saved some of the nature shots you did under other file names. Generic stuff just in case we needed them as leads for other stories. They were all gone. They had nothing to do with the story. They were just on the same reel."

"Did you ask Mangrove about it?"

"Of course. He claims he had no idea what happened to the files and reel. He tried to insinuate we screwed up the equipment check-in procedure. After how many years? We could both check-in equipment in our sleep."

"How did he act?"

"Like a weasely, little sycophant."

"Did he seem nervous or guilty?"

"How could I tell? The man is about as useful as the Pope's balls."

Roger bowed his head and chuckled to himself. No matter how many times he heard the line, it still made him smile. Maybe because Echo was the only person who said it. Gutsy women with great one-liners were anything if not appealing. The line also perplexed him. Roger could never think of a good response. The field was mined with priests and pedophile jokes, but nothing ever came to mind.

"So, we're here at the sheriff's station for the original report?"

"Right."

"And we don't just ask the sheriff for it because . . ."

"I don't want anyone to know we are looking for it."

Echo and Roger crept towards the door. Both crowded into the space between the wall and the decorative shrubbery. Roger squeezed past Echo to get to the doorknob. He pulled out a small toolkit and unzipped it. He grabbed the door handle to steady himself while he adjusted himself on the balls of his feet.

Click.

Roger and Echo exchanged dumbfounded looks. She quickly opened the door, and pushed Roger into the station. "Roger, when was the last time you heard of the sheriff's station left unlocked?"

"I grew up here. It's probably the only door that has always been locked."

"I think I know who did it."

The two split up and went through the station. Roger called out to Echo, "Hey. The hard drives from the computers are gone."

Echo called back, "And I can't find the report the campers made. The only report I can find is the Dickover sighting." She stood up, and turned to Roger. Indicating over her shoulder, "Did you know there are four filing cabinets full of Elvis literature? Alphabetized by year since his birth?"

"You have met Sheriff Paan before?"

"I know. What's weird is the files on Elvis end on December 21, 1970, but Elvis didn't die until 1977. He also has the period from 1971 to 1977 labeled as 'The Impostor Years'."

"Sheriff Paan believes Elvis was assassinated on December 21, 1970, four days before Christmas. And that an impostor was used to replace him. He believes it was the impostor who died the summer of 1977."

"Well, that explains this," Echo replied, producing a worn newspaper clipping from 1970. The picture on the clipping shows a smiling President Nixon shaking Elvis's hand in the Oval Office. Behind the two men, against the wall, are a line of flag poles. Each pole draped with the flag of a U.S. State.

Clipped to the article is the uncropped, original photograph of the photo in the newspaper article. In the uncropped version, two men dressed completely in black can be seen flanking Elvis and President Nixon. Echo immediately recognizes the two men as the ones who broke into her apartment. Except they haven't aged a day. She flips the photo over. The acronym 'R.I.P.' is written in the sheriff's handwriting on the back.

"How long have you known the sheriff?

"I went all through school with him. He's always been that way. Even back in elementary," Roger said, correctly enunciating the 'tary' in elementary. Locals didn't truncate the suffix to 'tree' like the rest of the country did. "He always said he was Elvis reincarnated. He took a lot of ribbing about it back in school. Kids can be hard."

"It is kind of like painting a bull's eye on your chest."

"True, but he's a good guy."

Echo pushed the implications of the men in the picture, and began digging through the office white paper recycling bin for the report when she saw piece of paper behind the bin. "Hey, look at this."

"Is it our report?"

"No. It's another report. They must've missed this one."

After reading the report, Echo and Roger's eyes met. "Why is someone getting rid of all of the Bigfoot reports?" Roger asked.

"They aren't. All of them but the Dickover sighting. That report was exactly where it should be."

"Someone only wants us to report the Dickover sighting?"

"And they're suppressing the other sightings," Echo said as she headed out the door. "There's something going on here."

30

"A Man Needs a Maid"
~Neil Young

Jeff, Harry, Patch, and Deputy O'Boogie sat around Deputy O'Boogie's desk. A Monopoly game was opened on top of stacks of paperwork. Harry was shaking dice inside a white Tioga County Sheriff Department coffee cup stained by years of coffee. Patch had on a sheriff's deputy cowboy hat pushed back on his head. "I'll sell you Marvin Gardens if you agree to only charge me the rent without houses when I land on that whole stretch."

Jeff sat up bristling with serial-rule follower self-righteousness. "You can't make side deals in Monopoly."

"Why not?"

"It's not fair!"

"Hello? It's Monopoly! Monopolies aren't fair! That's the essence of the game. It's an acceptable way to kick your loved ones in the nuts on family game nights."

"I believe it is also against the rules."

"You should talk. You're the reason we're arrested. You carry illegal dart guns, but adhere to the rules of board games? If only the county's laws were written by Parker Brothers."

"Me? Your friend is the one who darted the sheriff."

"Shut up and play," interrupted Deputy O'Boogie.

"Winston, after this game, can we go look at the

evidence room again?" Patch asked.

"Why?"

"I don't know. I like when you tell me stories about the stuff."

"You know the stories! Half the stuff is Earl's!"

"I know. His versions of the stories are just angry. Yours are a lot funnier."

The conversation was interrupted by Sheriff Paan entering the office. He walked stiffly across the room. He pulled a chair to Deputy O'Boogie's desk. He laid an inflatable hemorrhoid ring on the chair's seat. He carefully centered himself over the ring before gingerly sitting down. Jeff, Harry, and Winston looked away during the process. Patch watched intently, cocking his head sideways to get a better view of buttocks to inflatable ring contact.

"How's do you know where to sit if you were hit in both cheeks?"

Sheriff Paan's mood improved only slightly since leaving the woods. He turned towards Jeff. "Well, we found your partner. Found that hound dog walking down the highway when a state trooper picked him up. He was walking the wrong way from town, damn near made it all the way to Pennsylvania."

"Oh, good. How was he?"

"He'll be all right. He was all shook up[17] and dehydrated. He probably could stand to have walked a few more pounds off. He's at your hotel now resting up."

Patch and Harry looked at each other. "So that must've been the fat guy we saw running through the woods."

---

[17] "All Shook Up", written by Otis Blackwell.

Jeff sighed. "That would be Roy. He's a fairly typical Bigfoot believer. He's has an encyclopedic knowledge of Bigfoot, but not much of a field researcher."

Deputy O'Boogie chimed in, "How do you become a Bigfoot researcher? I mean, why?"

"Have you ever seen a Bigfoot, before yesterday?" asked Harry.

"I'm not sure. I think I did. It's been so long ago. I was a young lieutenant in the Army stationed in South Carolina. My squad was on a three-day field training. An Army sponsored camping trip with guns. I wanted to make my mark, so I led my squad outside of our assigned sector. I wanted to flank the opposing force. I figured I could apply a little gamesmanship to the exercise. I was young and dumb. I reasoned the enemy wouldn't stay in an assigned sector for our convenience, so neither should we.

"So, I led my squad out of our sector into some pretty rough country; off the charts I was issued. I figured I had enough land navigation classes to be able to get us around to the opposing force's flank and back onto the map. What I didn't know was the Army purposefully withheld the maps. There were buried mineral deposits in the area which threw our compasses off. This was before GPS. The mineral deposits created a magnetic anomaly. North depended on where you were standing. Some places, the compasses needle just spun around. If we held the compass sideways, the needle would point straight down. I figured it was because the needle was slightly heavy because of the magnet on it. I didn't know the needle was being pulled down by the magnetic field. Needless to say, I experienced a field commander's worst nightmare: I had gotten my squad lost."

"You were still in North America. How lost could you be?" asked Winston.

"Unfortunately, being on foot, the anomaly's effect was so gradual we didn't notice it. We traveled at night so we didn't have the sun to give us a celestial navigation reboot. There's the North Star, but it is only north-ish. It doesn't lie directly on magnetic or true north from our position, so it wasn't unusual to be slightly off from its position. It wasn't until the next day did I accept the truth of the situation. I decided to set up camp on a hill side. The area was heavily wooded, but offered a good vantage point of the exercise area we were supposed to be working in. The plan was to wait until morning, then return to our assigned sector. Hopefully, with a little luck, nobody would know about our little excursion. I ordered camp set up according to U.S. Army field manuals, complete with sentries, patrols, the works."

Jeff sat up in his chair and shifted nervously. He began rubbing his hands excessively and rocking in his chair; nervous tics animating his body.

"That night, we had some incidents." Jeff looked up to see everyone leaning forward, intently listening to him. He shifted his gaze back to the floor and continued. "Initially, it was nothing to speak of. Just a feeling. A sense we weren't alone. Infantry soldiers, as a whole, are the type to investigate these things. Years of being told we were a premier fighting force, tip of the spear, all the macho clichés. It made us cocky and overconfident. So, when things started happening, we charged in. Nothing could mess with us, especially in our own country.

"Like I said, at first nothing tangible had happened, but the roving sentries paired up to investigate some strange sounds. When I was notified, the sergeant had

155

the squad on alert. The sentries had reported strange noises nearby. Twigs snapping, heavy breathing; that sort of thing. When the sentries returned without finding anything, I had the squad stand down. The last thing I needed was a bunch of kids getting spooked in the woods.

"About three in the morning, the assault came. Large rocks and logs were thrown into the camp, raining down on us from the woods. The assault seemed to be coming from everywhere. I had the sergeant conduct a quick head count. I assumed it was one of the young soldiers playing a prank. Taking advantage of the spookiness of the evening. When the sergeant reported everyone was accounted for was about the same time the rocks flying at us were getting bigger and the aim was getting accurate.

"We had firearms. It was the Army; you didn't go anywhere without a rifle. But we were in an exercise, so we hadn't been issued ammunition. All of our rifles had these orange barrel plugs to indicate we couldn't shoot anyone. The Army figured civilians would feel better about having a gun pointed at them with an orange thing plugging the barrel. I ordered the plugs removed. I figured whoever was raiding us would take us more seriously if they thought we were armed."

Jeff paused to take a drink of water out of a loaner coffee cup. He made a slight face from the coffee aftertaste.

He cleared his throat and continued, "Assuming an armed posture didn't help. The rocks raining down were getting more accurate and there were some casualties. Whoever was throwing the rocks seemed to have developed a tactic against us: large rocks to hit tents and equipment, small rocks to hit us. We were being hit by softball sized rocks. They were really taking their toll on us. Some of the younger soldiers took to batting the rocks with their rifles. The rock thrower took to lobbing two rocks in succession at those soldiers. That took out my Babe Ruth's. I ordered a retreat. I needed a minute to regroup and figure out what was going on.

"I decided to turn aggressor. I mean, we were America's premier fighting force, right? We couldn't be chased off by a bunch of kids throwing rocks. I split the squad evenly, having my sergeant lead a frontal attack while took the other half to flank the escape."

Jeff paused again, squeezing the bridge of his nose with his thumb and forefinger. He glanced at his audience, mumbled, and then covered his eyes with his hands.

"What happened?" asked Harry.

"It was horrible. A nightmare. I lost a lot of good men that day."

"They were killed?" asked Winston.

"No. No deaths, but some of those young men will never enter the woods again for the rest of their lives."

"What happened?"

"Not 'what;' who? It was everywhere. It came at us from every direction."

"'It'?"

Jeff nodded affirmation, "It was a trap. It had planned the whole thing out. We walked right into it. All my training, all of our training; it hadn't prepared us for that."

"For?"

"It . . ." Jeff stammered, "It threw feces at us. There was piles of it. It's aim was uncanny. It was in our eyes, ears, noses, . . . it was in our mouths."

"Are you kidding?" asked Harry.

Jeff looked him with red-rimmed eyes and a look

of sorrow, "I . . . wiped my eyes, and silhouetted by the moon light was . . . this big, hairy . . . thing."

"Bigfoot?"

"I honestly don't know."

"What did the Army say?"

"It didn't. We were individually visited by some men. These guys weren't regular army; government types. Probably spooks. They threatened us to never talk about what happened. Like any of us would."

"Who do you think they were?"

"Don't know. Just three men dressed in identical black suits."

31

"You Know You're Right"
~Nirvana

Earl listened to snoring behind him. Earl hadn't ever heard anything snore so loud. It sounded like a flatulent grizzly bear swallowed a diesel engine and was trying to start it by doing Kegels. Earl's only experience with snoring since leaving home was with women. Even the drunken, sleep apnea suffering, overweight, chain-smoking girls he brought home from the Beaver didn't sound like this. Their tequila snores were cute purrs in comparison. Earl was annoyed the ape was sleeping next to him, and snoring loud enough to wake him up. He fought the urge to tell the ape to roll over on his stomach.

Earl had been able to move his arms and legs for several hours. After he'd tried to call for help, the horny apeman came to check on him. Earl pretended to be still knocked out or asleep, whatever Boner McMonkey thought he was doing before. It had gotten so close, Earl could smell its putrid breath.

How the hell does that thing have such bad breath? Don't monkeys eat fruit and bananas?

Earl thought it was going to try to kiss him, but thankfully it left him alone.

I would not have been able to keep my cool if that thing stuck its tongue down my throat.

It did paw at Earl, but it seemed to only be checking on him. Then it curled up on a bed next to him and grunted and groaned. It sounded sort of like a lullaby sung by a polar bear getting its nuts crushed.

Earl sat up and looked around. He was inside some sort of den filled with camping gear. Sleeping bags and tents were piled in a corner. Logs used as makeshift shelves held lanterns, water bottles, and compasses. It looked like someone had robbed a camping outfitter. There was one opening with logs laid over a support beam wedged between two large oaks, a primitive lean-to. The structure wasn't natural, but probably looked that way from the outside. Logs fell and got stacked up all over the forest in a similar pattern.

He could see light from the three quarter moon partially illuminating his escape. The ape lay on its side snoring between him and freedom. Earl quietly stepped over the narrowest part of the slumbering giant, its head. When Earl had a foot planted on each side of the apeman's head, the ape snorted loudly. Earl jumped, banging his head into a log overhead. The apeman had stopped snoring. Earl stood stooped over with ass dangling in inches from the ape's nose. Earl braced himself on a log and looked between his legs. A huge grin was plastered on its face, but it's eyes were closed. Earl sighed. Then he noticed he was in the sixty-nine position with Boner McMonkey. Earl quietly lifted his leg and crept out of the den.

Clear of the den, Earl quietly moved along until he was sure he was out of earshot. The snoring had started again and was fully chugging along. When he could no longer hear the snoring, Earl stopped to get his bearings. Earl pulled off the Chewbacca mask and welcomed the cool air on his face. He'd been sweating excessively inside the suit. Now, every movement wafted truck-stop bathroom up through the costumes neck hole. Earl reached into the Chewbacca purse for his Bluetooth headset, and placed it in his ear. Finally,

Earl reluctantly put the mask back on; just in case Boner McMonkey found him again. He did not want it to find out he wasn't another Bigfoot.

The conclusion had not come easily to Earl.

Earl found himself in a part of the woods he wasn't familiar with. By the light of the moon, he thought he could make out a familiar ridge in the distance. Except the ridge features were reversed from his memory because he was on the other side, several valleys over from his truck. If Earl was reading the terrain right, there should be a small mountain stream which eventually leads to the river. He could follow the river all the way to town.

Earl began down the trail in a half jog / half power walk, whatever the terrain and moonlight would allow. Soon, he could hear the soft buzz of the stream. Inside the mask, the sound of the stream sounded like the woods was shushing him. The sound of water made him realize how dehydrated he was. Earl quickened his pace.

The sound of the stream grew louder. Even in the mask, Earl could make out the individual splishes and splashes. His foot slipped on a wet stone and Earl slid down the bank into the stream. Freezing water rushed inside the costume through the holes in the face mask and neck. Earl lifted his head out of the water, allowing more water to rush down the neck hole. The water was painful against Earl's skin. His body was overheated, the sudden temperature change shocked his system; an aquatic bed of nails slapping his nerve endings with an ice cream headache. Earl lay there drinking his fill, and letting the water flood over him. Then he pissed in the suit again and craned his neck to allow the more water in to rinse it out. When he was satisfied with the rinse job, he slogged out of the stream, carefully dumping any water trapped in the suit.Earl adjusted the mask and began moving down stream, careful to avoid the steep bank in the dim light. Erosion and beavers had knocked down most of the big trees along the bank, creating a natural trail.

Just as Earl was finding his pace again, three men in dark suits stepped out onto the trail in front of him.

32

"I Ain't Hiding"
~The Black Crowes

Three men in identical business suits confronting a man dressed as Chewbacca in the middle of the woods was like a costume party gone bad. This rabbit hole led to the Land of the Inappropriately Dressed.

Earl skidded to a stop at the sight of the three men. He was naturally distrustful of anyone who wore a suit. While the rest of America viewed a suit and tie as the silk and wool watermark of a successful man. Earl viewed the clothes as the mark of a loser. A sheep in wuss's clothing. Suits were for douche bags on an anal-retentive authority trip. So concerned with fitting in that they were afraid to cut it in the real world. Like Earl did. Earl had money for beer each night and gas in the car. There was always a bar fly interested in being seduced by just such a man as him. His hatred of suits and ties began with the school principals and truancy officers of his past, to the lawyers and probation officers of his present. Something told him by the look of these three, these suits weren't going to have anything positive for his future. "Who the fuck are you?"

The tallest man stepped forward and began speaking in grunts and clicks. The language sounded identical to Bigfoot's. The speech seemed to emanate from the man instead of projected from the mouth, although the man's mouth moved when he spoke. Sort of like he was lip-syncing to an audio track of bears mating. Earl cocked his head at the freaky blow: he was deep in the woods, late at night, and men in business suits were speaking Bigfootese.

The tallest Dark Agent turned to the other two suits. "This solves the mystery of the additional *Gigantopithecus* in this sector. That . . . " gesturing at Earl " . . . is a man in a Chewbacca costume." Turning back to Earl, "Now, my little, foul mouthed friend, tell me what you think you are doing."

Earl diffused the situation the best way he knew how, "Go fuck yourself, Skeletor."

The tallest Dark Agent smiled broadly. A charming gesture but the overall effect was unsettling. "It is ironic a Chewbacca costume got you into this mess. Did you know the Chewbacca character was based on George Lucas's dog, an Alaskan Malamute? Are you familiar with the breed? Looks similar to a husky. Big, furry sled dogs with white, silver, and black coats. A handsome animal, really. A very different look than the creature shown in the films. I don't believe the character would have been as believable if he had white and silver hair. It doesn't really suit the characterization of a smuggler copilot. The shaggy, brown, and black coat fits the rogue persona better, in my opinion.

"Fortunately for Mr. Lucas, his timing was impeccable. At the time Mr. Lucas began filming his opus, *Star Wars*, there was a rash of Bigfoot sightings. America was gripped by Bigfoot mania. After 1967, when the *Patterson-Gimlin* film was released . . . I take it by the blank look on your face that you are either dimwitted or you have never heard of the Patterson-Gimlin film. It is the famous footage of a Bigfoot walking in California. No? How are you a Bigfoot hoaxer and you are not even aware of potentially the greatest Bigfoot hoax ever pulled? That is, depending which side of the Bigfoot camp you stake your claim on. The film is simultaneously credited as indisputable proof of Bigfoot. Interesting how the same film proves and disproves the existence of Bigfoot, depending on the viewer's beliefs. A polarity of views of the same thing has always been the problem with humans. Evidence planted as, what you might call a red herring, an attempt to influence and distract humans from something we would rather not have the public aware of. The problem is: for every piece of disinformation laid, there will be numerous, conflicting interpretations.

"Prior to yesterday, I am guessing you did not believe in Bigfoot. Why else would you prance around the woods dressed as one? I suppose, in light of recent events, your opinion has been profoundly altered on the matter." The tallest Dark Agent added with a smirk, "Perhaps, now you can be an expert witness on the validity of the film."

Earl shifted on the drywaller's stilts. The bubbling fountain of useless trivia was just confusing him. He also didn't like that they knew of his capture. Earl needed a drink and he needed to get out of the monkey suit. Chatting with some suits late at night in the woods wasn't helping him get either one. "What's the point, Skeletor?"

Ignoring Earl's rudeness, the tallest Dark Agent continued, "In the mid 1970s, the United States government approached me to begin naturalizing all of the Bigfoots, or Bigfeet. Your government has never settled on what shall be the plural form of Bigfoot. I was tasked with the naturalization process for the resident Bigfeet within your country's borders. A task which must be done with care. Humans, as a whole, do not do well when anything is presented which conflicts with long-standing ideologies and beliefs regarding religion, evolution, zoology. Coupled with that new evidence would be the glaring fact that while you collectively had been flag waving for your rights to light beer and pre-distressed jeans, large bipeds–distant cousins in an evolutionary sense–had been living in your backyard. I can hear your country's talking heads saber-rattling against whatever political party was currently wielding the political conch that they failed. Not only to secure the border and keep out the immigrants, but they also missed the fact that thousands of giant primates were living in every corner of the country. Despite the fact the Bigfeet lived on these lands long before *Homo Sapien* set foot on this continent. Your defense and law enforcement agencies would have raised the Bigfoot's pelt as a reason for more funding. Every political party would be courting them as constituents. The liberals would want to expand the welfare state to include them. It would have been a mess. Not to mention humans tend to react violently whenever anything disrupts their worldview, or distracts them from the televisions and strip malls."

Earl clung to the parts of the speech he understood. "So, you're feds?"

"No. I have been employed by your government on a–we should call it a 'consulting' basis, but we do not belong to any branch of your, or any other country's government.

I decided to introduce the Bigfeet, their correct name is *Gigantopithecus*, slowly to the American culture. Here's where Mr. Lucas's timing could not have been better. I paid Mr. Lucas a visit early during the initial production of *Star Wars*. Then I persuaded, really guided, Mr. Lucas to alter his vision of Han Solo's loyal copilot, and the rest, as you say, is history.

I am sure you have noticed the physical similarities between Bigfoot and Chewbacca. What is more important, Chewbacca needed to be likable. Something humans, particularly Americans, could be drawn to; a loyal companion, a fierce friend. For Mr. Lucas's integrity in taking my redirection–not that he had a choice–I ensured his film was made, despite Fox's budget problem. Money was found and earmarked for Mr. Lucas. Why, you may ask, would I go through such trouble? To begin desensitizing the American public to Bigfoot. That movie was the first shot of the United States government's plan to naturalize not just the Bigfeet, but all the creatures which fall outside of your awareness. Remember the cantina scene in the movie? Every creature we planned to naturalize was represented in the bar."

"So what happened? Why aren't the Bigfoots . . . feets . . . Bigfeetses naturalized? Why aren't they living with us? Because I always wanted a Chewbacca when I was a kid."

"Ah, sadly, as what often happens in a democracy. The regimented, peaceful handover of power. A new president was elected with a new political agenda. It's really why I've always like monarchies. You can count on your government's word when it's the same face year after year.

The P.L.A.N. withered on the vine and now we are tasked with keeping those Things That Go Bump In the Night from revealing themselves too early before we can systematically implement the naturalization plan for them."

"So, you're responsible for *Harry and the Hendersons*?

"No. That was your government's attempt to carry out my plan without me. That film was essentially a

US government training film for children."

"It sucked."

"I agree it was not up to my standard. Not to mention the breach of contract on your government's part. I sell my services, not my plans. Fortunately, those responsible for the film were suitably punished."

"*Star Wars* sucked, too."

"Perhaps films are not your forte."

"You know what's also not my forte? Standing around in the woods talking to sci-fi nerds." Earl attempted to resume down the trail, chest-bumping the tallest Dark Agent out of his way. Earl bounced off the slight man. It felt like he bumped into a concrete light post. Earl was shocked the man was ice cold. Even the suit and surrounding air was frigid. It was as if the strange man had his own personal ecosystem. A body proactively creating its own comfort zone, instead of a body reacting to the environment with constricting blood vessels and sweat glands.

The other two agents did not react to Earl's attempts.

Earl cocked his arm back to straight arm him out of his way. The tallest Dark Agent's hand shot out and grabbed Earl's hand, dislocating Earl's thumb in the process. The tallest Dark Agent held Earl's hand and sneered. "You would recognize this as the part of the movie -if you watched any movies- where the antagonist explains to the hero; you are to be the hero in this production -a role I imagine you are certainly unfamiliar with and definitely undeserving of- that you know too much. I suspect you being accused of knowing too much is another trait you are unaccustomed to. The antagonist then explains that because of this knowledge, the hero cannot be freed. I am inclined to make an exception in this case. I do not believe anything I have told you penetrated that solid rock you call a skull. However, you have been extremely rude and insulting, which I have only allowed because I knew you would not have much longer to practice your vulgar ways. I am a humanitarian in that way. I hope you enjoyed it." The tallest Dark Agent reached inside his jacket and withdrew an ancient flintlock pistol.

As the tallest Dark Agent pointed the weapon at Earl, a large rock, four times the size of a basketball, slammed into his head. The other two Dark Agents spun towards their attacker, drawing their side arms as they moved. A large spear impaled the first agent. The fence-post-thick spear was thrown with enough force to pass completely through the agent. The second agent was clotheslined by a thick wooden club, shattering the agent's skull. Bigfoot ran out of the woods, scooping Earl up in a fireman's carry without breaking stride.

The tallest Dark Agent stood up. He irritatedly fixed his hair and shucked his cuffs. Sickening cracks accompanied the caved in eye socket and cheek bones audibly repairing themselves. Vertebrae healed and realigned themselves, allowing the agent to hold his head up again; his neck doing an impression of a slinky returning to its compressed form.

Four agents stepped onto the trail. Two picked up the dead agents and withdrew into the woods. The other two agents were identical to the two dead agents. The Tallest Dark Agent's neck made grinding noises as he turned to inspect the two agents. "I do not know what is going on with that fucking ape."

33

"Bastards of Young"
~The Replacements

Sheriff Paan entered the station's cell block. A water balloon flopped like a fat tit into the door and plopped on the floor, where it rolled towards a floor drain. Laughter and catcalls erupted when the dud failed to break. Patch dashed to the balloon, pausing to wave at the sheriff and dashed off to rejoin the fight. Deputy Winston O'Boogie slid across the wet floor carrying a squirt gun the size of a scuba tank, slamming himself into a cell wall, then altering course after Patch. Harry jumped out of another cell armed with two obscene, lunch-lady breast-sized water balloons cradled in each arm. He stopped in the middle of the hallway, fixed his eyes on the sheriff and bellowed, "Get him!".

"Hold 'er right there, partner", Sheriff Paan commanded. "Don't ya'll want to get outta here and find Earl?"

Harry paused and shrugged. "Yes. We can still look for him if you're wet."

"Boys, you're free to go. You've been bailed out. You don't need to rock this jailhouse no longer."

Patch looked at Deputy O'Boogie, "We were still in jail?"

"You were. You're free to go now. Roy bailed Jeff out. Harry, Domino bailed you and Patch out." Fixing an accusing on Harry, "Son, you'd better pick up a tube of Chapstick on the way home; you've got some serious ass to kiss ahead of you."

34

"Cold Water"
~Tom Waits

Harry mulled over his options all the way to Domino's. She was pissed and poorer; whatever the damage was for springing he and Patch out of the clink. He reasoned she couldn't be too pissed if she was still bailing him out. There was still a silver lining there, but not without one big thunderstorm of angry blonde. He already knew the trajectory of the argument. Not that it was going to help him, like being able to predict the specific face values of a losing hand.

He just wanted to skip to the end of the argument. Once, he'd suggested just that when he heard the familiar choir warming up (*You need to change, uh huh, uh huh*). "Look, let's just pretend you bitched at me about whatever I did to get a thumb in your butt. We'll just fast-forward to the part where we exchange 'fuck you's', and let the punishing silent treatment begin."

The realization that he should've kept that little suggestion to himself was punctuated by Domino's fist. Funny how a boyfriend hitting his girlfriend ruins his reputation, when her slugging him improves hers.

All of their arguments seemed to lead to the same exit: exiled from the wondrous wonders of vagina-land. She said a bunch of other stuff too, but Harry only focused on the physical punishment. Bitching, moaning, and groaning could be tuned out. Hot nights on cold shoulders were harder to ignore.

Without his recognition, Domino's complaining

had taken a foothold on his conscience. Like waves pounding the shore into a new shape, her desires and needs were sinking in. There just wasn't enough influence to change his behavior. Lately she blasted away at his columns of bachelorhood with a three-pronged attack for stability, maturity, and matrimony. What Harry got out of the conversations was there was a lot of biological clock clanging, eggs getting dusty, and partner-suitability evaluations going on. The other part getting clearer to Harry was it was his fault, and he was ending up as the loser in a one person contest. Harry pounded the steering wheel in frustration. Domino used to be satisfied with him, maybe even happy with him. Now she wanted things. Bigger things than drinking and sex and hanging out. She had a destination in mind. A vision she was trying to share, but he couldn't see it. It was false advertising! She can't be satisfied with him one day, more than satisfied, she fell in love with him. Then decide he was not enough. She can't order a hamburger, and then expect it to become a steak after three bites. His needs hadn't changed, why did hers? Why couldn't it be like the old days?

Harry would have to handle the situation perfectly. He couldn't just walk into Domino's. The trap was set, and the spider was waiting. He had to enter the wolf's lair on his terms. Fortunately Harry was a master of deflective entrance. The art was changing the situation to where she was reacting to his actions, instead of launching into the *you're an asshole* monologue she'd been muttering to herself for the last two hours. It all comes down to the first few moments of walking through the door.

Mostly, he needed to find Earl. He didn't have time to go through Domino's entire dissertation on his inadequacies as a boyfriend.

Maybe there's an abridged version. I'll remember to get out of punching range before I ask for that. Fortunately, this situation doesn't require a lie. As long as she buys the story.

Harry grabbed the doorknob and took a deep breath. *It all comes down to the first few moments.* Harry flung open the door, and sprinted across the living room. Domino, arms crossed, blocked his path. *She makes a big obstacle for a girl her size.*

"Baby, I've got to get . . ."

"Not this time. We aren't playing your games, buster."

"But . . ." Harry continued, his resolve weakened. "Really, this time . . ."

Domino reached up and flicked his nose. "No," she said in a tone reserved for puppies. "Sit."

Harry threw himself onto the couch. He crossed his arms and tapped his foot. He was really annoyed she was using dog-training techniques on him.

Domino began pacing the living room. She flapped her hands at her sides, and grumbled to herself. After her fifteenth lap she turned to face her boyfriend. "You've done a lot of things which have pissed me off. I've tried. I've really tried to accept your shortcomings. I've forgiven you for all of the crappy things you've done to me. And, buddy, there's been plenty. Do I need to mention the time you tie-dyed my silk sheets in my bathtub? The porcelain is still stained, and no, it doesn't look 'groovy.' I've forgiven you for wrecking my car. And the time you got my nieces stoned. The time you posted naked pictures of me on the internet. The time you shot all of my Christmas ornaments with a BB gun. The time you shaved our initials into my cat's fur. The time you farted at Christmas dinner with my family, and then tried to high-five my mother. The time you spiked the sangria for my Girls-Only-Wine-Night hoping it would descend into a lesbian orgy. Insisting we have sex on bubble wrap. The time you asked me to hum the theme to *Star Wars* during a blow-job. Should I go on?" She spun to face Harry, who responded by shaking his head. "I've tried to accept the drinking, the pot smoking, the questionable hygiene, the utter lack of domestication, the inconsideration, the lack of any desire to get a real job. I really have. This time, this time, I can't accept it."

"Look, I'll pay you back for bailing us out."

"I'm not talking about that. You really are the dumbest man in the world. I've told all of my friends. You need to know that. When you're drunk and hitting on my girlfriends, they know you are the dumbest man in the world. No, this time I'm talking about you and your brain-damaged friends harassing my patients!"

For the first time in their relationship, Domino's tone scared him. He began to wonder what he would do without her. His brain kicked into overdrive, searching for something to say to defuse the bomb. Her accusation rocked him back into the room. Harry cocked his head quizzically at her. This time it wasn't an act.

"What are you talking about?"

"Don't play innocent with me. The patients are talking about Bigfoot. One of my patients- my patient, Harry-thinks he smokes cigarettes with Bigfoot. This time you've gone too far. Those people need help. They don't need to be made fun of."

Harry jumped up. "Baby, it isn't us. That's what I'm talking about. That thing has Earl."

"Stop it. Just stop it. I don't believe you." Domino

stopped in front of the stereo, and began shuffling through his Pearl Jam CDs. She punched the stereo on; not finding the song she needed, she mashed the 'off' button. Domino resumed flapping her hands in frustration.

She's at a loss for words. She's going to channel Pearl Jam. That's bullshit. She can't do the speaking in tongues to one of my bands. She doesn't even like them.

"You can't bitch at me via my favorite band. You have to find another band to channel."

Domino turned to face him, her face and body contorting with emotion straining on an invisible leash. *"Waiting, watching the clock. It's four o'clock. It's got to stop. Tell him; take no more. She practices her speech. As he opens the door, she rolls over..."*[18]

"No! Domino. You can't do Pearl Jam. Every time I hear their songs, it will no longer remind me of college! It will remind me of breaking up. You are ruining grunge!"

She lifts her eyes to look into his. The intensity of the look knocks him back both physically and emotionally; the demon of angst spitting the bridle out of her mouth. She wasn't just channeling Pearl Jam. She was channeling the band's lead singer, Eddie Vedder, circa 1992.

"Talking to herself, there's no one else who needs to know. She tells herself; memories back when she was bold and strong, and waiting for the world to come along. Swears she knew it, now she swears he's gone. She lies and says she's in love with him. Can't find a better man. She dreams in color, she dreams in red. Can't find a better man. She lies and says she still loves him. Can't find a better man..."[19]

---

[18] "Better Man", written by Eddie Vedder.
[19] "Better Man", written by Eddie Vedder.

"Honey, don't do this."

"Is there room for both of us? Both of us apart? Are we bound by obligation? Is that all we've got?"[20]

"No. That's not all we . . ."

"The waiting drove me mad. You're finally here, and I'm a mess. I take your entrance back. Can't let you roam inside my head. I don't want to take what you can give. I would rather starve than eat your bread. I would rather run, but I can't walk. Guess I'll lay alone just like before"[21]

"Domino, this isn't fair. Pearl Jam doesn't have any let's-just-be-happy-and-chill-your-girlfriend-out lyrics. They're all something-is-wrong songs."

"She once believed in every story he had to tell. One day she stiffened, took the other side. Empty stares from each corner of a shared prison cell. One just escapes. One's left inside the well. And he who forgets will be destined to remember . . . nothingman."[22]

Harry's mental-digging around for lyrics struck something solid. He grasped at it, *"Gonna save you, fucker, not gonna lose you. Feeling cocky and strong, can't let you go. Too important to me . . ."*[23]

Domino cut him off, *"First comes love, then comes pain. Let the games begin."*[24]

Harry pushed on while he searched for something to soothe her with, *". . . Too important to us, we'd be lost without you. Baby, let yourself fall. I'm right below you now. And fuck me if I say something you don't wanna hear. And fuck me if you only hear what you wanna hear. Fuck me if I care, but I'm not leaving*

[20] "Hail, Hail", written by Eddie Vedder.
[21] "Corduroy", written by Eddie Vedder and Pearl Jam.
[22] "Nothingman", written by Eddie Vedder.
[23] "Save You", written by Eddie Vedder.
[24] "Love Boat Captain", written by Eddie Vedder.

here"[25]

"Don't even think about reaching me. I won't be home. Don't even think about stopping by. Don't think of me at all. I did what I had to do. If there was a reason, it was you."[26]

"I've used hammers made out of wood. I have played games with pieces and rules. I've deciphered tricks at the bar, but now you're gone. I haven't figured out why. I've come up with riddles and jokes about war. I've figured out numbers and what they're for. I've understood feelings and I've understood words, but how could you be taken away?"[27]

"Don't gimme no lip."[28]

Harry took the short response from Domino as a good sign. Maybe she was running out of lyrics. He pressed on, hoping to gain some ground with her, "There's a light when my baby's in my arms. There's a light when the window shades are drawn. Hesitate when I feel I may do harm to her. Wash it off 'cause this feeling we can share, and I know she's reached my heart, in thin air."[29]

"Seen it happen to a couple of friends. Seen it happen, and the message it sends. Taken up for what's an obvious fault. Just to see what all the fuss is about. It's not your way. Another habit says it's in love with you. Another habit says it's long overdue. Another habit like an unwanted friend."[30]

Harry found the lyrics that probably meant the most to him. The lyrics that captured his rage against

---

[25] "Save You", written by Eddie Vedder.
[26] "Footsteps", written by Eddie Vedder.
[27] "Light Years", written by Eddie Vedder.
[28] "Don't Gimme No Lip", written by Stone Gossard.
[29] "Thin Air", written by Stone Gossard.
[30] "Habit", written by Eddie Vedder.

her need for more, *"Fuck, be content to just get by. Why be satisfied? We've got all night."*[31]

"I wanna shake. I wanna wind out. I wanna leave this mind and shout. I've lived all this life like an ocean in disguise. I don't live forever. You can't keep me here"[32]

"I wish I was a messenger and all the news was good. I wish I was the full moon shining off your Camaro's hood. I wish I was the souvenir you kept your house key on. I wish I was the pedal brake that you depended on. I wish I was the verb 'to trust' and never let you down."[33]

Domino looked at Harry without speaking in tongues, "I wish you did too."

One last Pearl Jam lyric came to Harry. A lyric without fight or need for forgiveness, *"I miss you already."*[34]

They looked at each other for a long moment. One feeling the shock and anxiety of starting her life again. The other needing his friend more than ever. Both wondering how to break the moment, and secretly wanting it to last a little longer.

"I shot the sheriff[35]," Harry said, shifting to Bob Marley.

"What?"

"But I didn't shoot no deputy." [36]

"Get out."

"That isn't Bob Marley."

"I said, get the fuck out!"

---

[31] "All Night", written by Eddie Vedder and Pearl Jam.
[32] "Can't Keep", written by Eddie Vedder.
[33] "Wishlist", written by Eddie Vedder.
[34] "Smile", written by Eddie Vedder.
[35] "I Shot the Sheriff", written by Bob Marley.
[36] "I Shot the Sheriff", written by Bob Marley.

35

"Voodoo Candle"
~Son Volt

Harry moped back into the sheriff station. He stopped in the middle of the office, and stared blankly ahead. "It's over. She left me."

"Who left you?" Roy replied.

Harry turned to the new voice, "You're the fat guy we saw running away in the woods."

Roy looked down, "Yeah, sorry about that. I did come back, but you guys were already gone." Shifting gears, Roy walked over extending his hand, "You're the guy who shot the sheriff."

"Yes, that's the sonofabitch." Sheriff Paan answered, carrying his hemorrhoid doughnut with him. "Come on in, Harry. We've been waiting for you."

"Sheriff, Domino left me."

"Don't worry, son. You'll have plenty of time to get her back after we rescue Earl." Turning to the Sasquatch researchers, "Okay, gentlemen, let's begin."

Roy walked to the center of the room, and launched into a well-rehearsed speech, "Thank you, Sheriff Paan. What we think we're dealing with here is an authentic *Bipedus giganticus* . . ."

"A what?" Patch interrupted.

Jeff took over, "Bigfoot."

Patch looked up, "No duh. We knew that. How do we get Earl back?

"Well, our original intention was to tranquilize it. Then conduct a thorough field investigation. We could still dart it. We'll get the samples we need, and extract your friend."

Sheriff Paan bobbed his head from side to side, mulling the idea over. "Something's been itching at me: both of your stories had men in suits. We just investigated a forced-entry where the suspects match the same description. What's the connection?"

Jeff looked at Roy, clearly uncomfortable, "They could be Dark Agents." Jeff was met with a room full of blank stares. "Men In Black?" Jeff asked.

"I like that movie," Patch said.

"Unfortunately, the movie doesn't capture their true nature. Some believe the films were part of a conspiracy to discredit the fringe of our society who believe in UFOs, etc."

"I'm not following," Deputy O'Boogie said.

"Dark Agents are believed to be, well, they are believed to be a variety of things. They appear to witnesses of unexplainable phenomena, such as UFOs . . ."

"And Bigfoot?" Sheriff Paan interrupted.

"Yes. They are reported to threaten or harass witnesses. In some cases they offer alternate, mundane explanations to whatever the witness believes they saw. Someone who sees a UFO is told they saw a weather balloon or meteorological phenomenon. A Bigfoot sighting is an escaped monkey or bear. If the offered explanation is not accepted, then the witness is threatened. In other cases, such as mine, the information is simply suppressed.

They've been reported since the '50s, but information was possibly suppressed before that. We began to really hear about them in the '60s, around the time the country was really beginning to question our government. Americans were no longer as pliable.

There's evidence, at least circumstantially, that they've been present in one form or the other since the beginning of history. From the suppression of scientific discoveries in medieval Europe to government conspiracies today. For people who believe things–or have seen things they shouldn't–the inquisitions are still going on."

"Why pay us to hoax Bigfoot?" asked Harry.

"Probably because you were hoaxing Bigfoot. We know at least one Bigfoot is in the area. If one of those individuals are discovered, then you'll be used as the scapegoat. The attention will be focused on you. Then either a connection will be manufactured linking your hoaxes to the actual sighting or, if you assert the actual sighting wasn't one of your hoaxes, then you'll be discredited to the point no one will believe anything you say."

"You sound like you've seen this before," said Deputy O'Boogie.

"We have. If they are here, all of us may be in danger."

"What do you mean?"

"Noncompliance hasn't always been tolerated. Some people have just disappeared."

"Hold on. This isn't China. American citizens can't just be disappeared," said Deputy O'Boogie.

"Remember what was on the table at Echo's? These boys were playing for keeps," said Sheriff Paan.

36

"The Revolution Starts Now"
~Steve Earle

Earl's stomach ached from bouncing along Bigfoot's shoulder. He didn't know how long he'd been carried, or how far they went. He felt like he'd been in a car accident. His kidneys ached, and he was fairly certain he was going to piss blood. Getting a piggy-back ride from a mythical creature isn't the best time to think. Now, leaning against a tree, the past few hours was knocking into Earl's brain like waves batting a buoy.

Earl's thumb throbbed inside the costume glove. Swelling had immobilized the digit. He adjusted himself to try to find a comfortable position. Finally, settling on cradling his arm in his lap.

Bigfoot grabbed his arm to inspect the limb. Earl cried out; flinching instinctively. The glove did not pull off. Earl's swollen hand filled the glove; giving the impression of real fur and skin. Bigfoot loosened his grip, but did not release Earl's arm. He then began to coo softly, like a mother to a child. He then pointed excitedly over Earl's shoulder. As Earl turned his head to see, Bigfoot popped the thumb back into place. Earl yelped. He jumped up, shielding his hand from Bigfoot. Then realized his thumb felt better. It took him a moment to shake the expectation it should've hurt a lot worse. He looked up at Bigfoot, and smiled inside the mask.

To Bigfoot, New She-Bigfoot was giving him the

same impassive expression she always had. Except this look was a little different. Something about her eyes seemed to smile. Bigfoot returned the smile. This time, New She-Bigfoot didn't flinch at the sight.

Earl nodded his head, then moved off a short distance in the woods. He wanted to see if he was getting cell phone reception. As he walked away, Earl glanced over his shoulder to see if Boner McMonkey was looking. Earl jumped when he saw Bigfoot standing directly behind him. Bigfoot waved. Earl rolled his eyes inside the mask, and moved further into the brush. Bigfoot followed. Earl waved Boner McMonkey off, as he backed away. Bigfoot took a step closer. Earl gave him the Diana Ross *Stop! In The Name Of Love* hand. Bigfoot paused, then stepped back one step. Earl took one step away; Bigfoot matched his movement. Earl gave the international I-Have-To-Pee sign. Boner McMonkey bobbed his head in understanding. He then turned around, and covered his eyes with a hairy paw. If Earl had been looking, he'd seen the hair on Bigfoot' cheeks stand on end; the *Gigantopithecus* blush.

With some privacy, Earl dug into the wookie purse, and retrieved the cell phone. Using his body to block Boner McMonkey's view, Earl flipped the phone open. He powered the phone on, and pressed the cell between his hands to muffle the chime the cell made when it turned on. Waiting for the phone to initialize, Earl remembered to pretend to be peeing. He debated on standing, and peeing on everything like he witnessed Bigfoot do numerous times. How does a female bigfoot pee? Earl assumed the squat he'd witnessed drunk girls do. He realized it was more difficult than it looked. Certainly not as easy as peeing and standing. Earl realized he really did need to pee. How am I going to pull this off without pulling down the costume? He sat there crouched until he heard the cell chime. After checking over his shoulder for Boner, he flipped open the phone, and nearly fell over when he noticed the icon indicating full reception.

Earl jumped when the phone beeped a missed calls alert. He glanced over his shoulder. Bigfoot pretended not to be watching. Earl's cell chirped the voicemail alert as he searched the menu options for the vibrate mode. Bigfoot hooted. Earl waved back. Earl sighed with relief when the cell buzzed to indicate missed text messages.

Next he attempted to activate the Bluetooth in his ear. He didn't dare remove the costume glove to activate the hands-free device. He wiggled his good hand into the form fitting mask, and tried to feel the *On* button through the glove. The Bluetooth chimed in his ear. He found Harry's number in his contact list, and hit *Send*.

Harry's voicemail asked him to leave a message. The call to Patch went directly to voicemail.

Earl closed the phone, and bumped the earpiece to put it in *Standby*. He returned the phone to the wookie purse. Bigfoot smiled as he returned. Bigfoot took a step closer as Earl approached. Bigfoot towered over Earl, causing Earl to shift uncomfortably. Earl had been the largest kid in school. The position bestowed him with abundant amounts of confidence at a young age. Now, he used his size to his advantage as an adult. He didn't like feeling like someone's petite girlfriend. Earl didn't know about the sexual dimorphism in the Bigfoot species; males tend to be larger than the females. Earl's size, while large for *Homo Sapien*, made him downright petite compared to a female Bigfoot. The subtle difference made him exotic in

Boner's eyes.

Bigfoot smiled, and made *How you doing?* eyebrows at Earl. Earl stepped back and instinctively covered his ass with his hands. Boner McMonkey made a laughing sound, scooped Earl up in a bear hug. Earl beat on Bigfoot's chest and shoulders with his fists, grunting from the effort. Boner set Earl down, and gave him a friendly chuck on the arm and pinched his cheek.

Earl stepped away. He needed time to think. He couldn't run off again, not with those freaks in suits running around in the woods. He needed to lead the apeman closer to his truck. Then Earl could make his getaway.

Earl began down the trail towards his truck. Boner hooted a question. Earl beckoned him to follow. Boner grunted, and shook his head. Earl continued to beckon; Boner shook his head vigorously. Boner pointed towards Earl's intended route, and grunted a long stream of vocalizations. Boner pointed in another direction, and grunted a less-guttural vocalization.

Maybe he thinks the suits are that direction. He crossed through the brush to Boner's trail. Bigfoot gestured for Earl to lead the way. As they moved down the trail, Earl thought he could feel Boner's eyes on his ass. He shifted the wookie purse to cover his butt, and tried to walk like a dude. Hoping a masculine walk would shut the horny apeman down. It was having the opposite effect, Earl's self-conscience stride and bashfulness only turned Boner on more.

Soon, the trail broke to the left, and paralleled a chain-link fence. Boner put his paw on Earl's shoulder, and guided him into thick brush near the fence. On the other side of the fence, Earl could make out several buildings. He recognized the hospital immediately.

Earl, Harry, and Patch used to snipe at the patients with paintball guns until a judge threatened to lock them in the hospital. They were not sure if the Criminally-Insane-Psychopathic-Sodomizing-Rapists-Stricken-With-Every-STD-Known-To-Man Wing really existed, but the judge had been persuasive enough for them to not push their luck. The game had lost some of its appeal when a short, fat man with a bad comb-over began masturbating when the phosphorescent carnage started. The boys tried to nail the masturbator in the junk, but only seemed to make the little man more excited.

Bigfoot bobbed his head and hooted. To Earl's surprise, a hoot was echoed back from across the fence. The responding call was not an echo or mimic of Bigfoot's call. The response was an effeminate "Hoot. Hoot." Earl peered through the bushes to see a man was sitting on a bench under a tree, and was now sashaying towards the fence. Earl crouched down in the bushes. Boner chuckled, and grunted at the approaching man.

"There you are, ya big brute," Ted said. He had moved on to a new personality. This one was a gay homophobe. Ted's character wasn't just flaming; it was an inferno. The effete accent was sweetly tinged with a southern accent. The result was the listener had a strange sensation the voice was exactly how they imagined Jesus Christ sounded.

The latest character grew from the barfly. The back story of this character was he'd met the previous character, the barfly, in a bar. The two had spent the night drinking. The homosexual spent the night trying to convince the barfly he was straight. The drunk barfly thought the gay man was a woman. Things got blurry from there.

A flaw in the character was Ted didn't know many homosexuals. The ones he did know weren't very effeminate at all, just regular guys. Without a person to model his character on, Ted went Hollywood over-the-top gay man.

The real problem for Ted was he acted out the entire scene, from bar to bedroom, in the middle of the cafeteria . . . during dinner. After the dinner-show, his therapist prescribed Ted some new meds. With the additional medication, Ted took over as the break room's official Uno dealer from Don. While angry with the demotion, Don enjoyed Ted's show; twice. Don was also upset Ted refused to act out the scene again.

Seeing Earl for the first time, Ted squealed: "Oh, who's your little friend? A girlfriend?" Turning to Earl, "Hello, I'm Ted. It is wonderful to finally meet you. I haven't seen this big, hairy beast in a few days." Ted leered at Bigfoot as he spoke, "You must have been keeping him busy."

Earl looked cautiously at the man with an ascot meticulously tied around his neck. He wished he had a paintball gun.

Boner pointed at Ted's jacket.

"Oh, I know! Hold your hairy horses," Ted said, exaggerating the inflections. Addressing Earl as he pulled out a pack of cigarettes, "He just can't wait to get a fag in his mouth!" Ted had changed his cigarettes to a coffin nail targeted towards women. "I really should quit, but I just love it."

Bigfoot frowned at the long, ultra-thin cigarette. He motioned for another cigarette. Ted lit another one, and handed it over. Bigfoot took a drag from the two cigarettes at the same time. He motioned again for another cigarette. Still not satisfied, they repeated the process again until he was smoking five cigarettes at the same time.

"Oh, he wants a thick one!" Ted squealed, "I know what you mean, honey."

Earl watched the episode unfolding in front of him with a disgusted look on his face. He made the I-gotta-pee dance again to Bigfoot, and headed deeper into the woods for some privacy. Bigfoot rolled his eyes at Ted and grunted. If the grunt was translated it would have been a sarcastically apologetic "Women."

When he was far enough away, Earl bumped the Bluetooth *On* as he dialed Patch's number. It took several tries. An observer would have thought he was trying to knock something lose in his head. Earl's mouth fumbled when Patch picked up the phone. He was caught off guard, expecting to get voicemail again. Earl realized he had no idea where to start.

"Patch, get me the fuck out of here." Earl whisper-hissed into the phone.

"Who is this?" Patch answered.

"You know who the fuck this is, goddammit."

"I know. Are you okay?"

"Am I okay? You fuckin' serious? I've been abducted by a horny apeman."

"We know. We think it believes you are its girlfriend. So, that's cool. Just tell me where you are."

"On what planet is this cool? This is not cool. Come get me. I'm at the insane asylum. Come get me now."

"Is the Bigfoot with you?"

"Yeah, he won't leave me alone."

"Okay, we're at the sheriff station. Sheriff wants to put you on speaker. Tell us everything that's going on."

After covering the events of the last twenty-four

hours, Earl's story was met with silence. "Are you there?"

Sheriff Paan answered, "We're here. There's something you need to know: we believe the suits are still hunting you and the creature. Second, don't let the Bigfoot find out you're human."

"Why? What will happen?" Earl asked, fear creeping into his voice.

"Well, there's the rub. We have no idea."

"So, it could be okay?"

"Yes, Earl. How would you react if you found out your date was not a woman?"

Earl eyed Ted, bent wrist resting on an out-thrown hip. "Yeah. It's not going to be okay."

"The good news is: we have a plan. Hide in the hospital, and we'll come and get you."

Earl nearly screamed into the phone, "No fucking way. I'm not going in there with all the freaks."

"Earl, if the suits are looking for you in the woods, then you need to get indoors."

"What about the freaks? What if they talk?"

"Hound dog[37], I think you're missing the point. It is a mental hospital," Sheriff Paan said, stressing every syllable. "Who's going to listen to them?"

Turning to see Ted mid-prance as he acted out a number from a musical he'd seen. "Sheriff, I don't know."

"Earl, one more thing: do whatever it takes to convince the creature you're a Bigfoot."

"Bullshit." Earl replied as he popped the Bluetooth back to standby.

After the phone call, the sheriff station was quiet

---

[37] "Hound Dog", written by Jerry Leiber and Mike Stoller.

except for the burbling and hissing of the coffee pot. They'd all been waiting for some sort of direction, a cosmic road sign to guide them. Now they had one. Each one of the men present had been marginalized in some way most of their lives. Beta males, not equipped for action. Each man looked around the room, steeling themselves while offering support to the others.

"Sheriff, does the hospital have padded rooms?" asked Jeff.

"Yep, they even have jail cells. They aren't used for the patients any more. They're maintained in case we have an overflow here. Why?"

"Sounds like a place to make a stand."

Sheriff Paan nodded in agreement, "Warden threw a party in the county jail[38]." Turning to Harry, "Looks like you'll be seeing Domino sooner than you thought."

---

[38] "Jailhouse Rock", written by Jerry Leiber and Mike Stoller.

37

"Ball and Biscuit"
~The White Stripes

Earl walked back to Ted and Boner McMonkey. Bigfoot had smoked his fill of coffin nails, and was nodding along as Ted described a man-scaping regimen that would make the giant look 'fabulous', and really bring out his eyes, which Ted described as 'as big as a unicorn's testicles'. Earl vomited a little in his mouth as Ted recommended trimming around Boner's crotch area to make his 'thingy' look bigger.

A bell rang from a loudspeaker mounted on the outside of the wall of one the buildings. Ted groaned, "That's me. Those fuckers won't leave me alone. A diva's work is never done." He sashayed away, beauty queen waving over his shoulder. "Ta-ta, kids. Tomorrow? Same bat-time, same bat-channel. I'll bring some conditioner for you."

Watching his entrance ticket prance away, Earl hooted. A passable impression of Bigfoot's call. Not sure what else to do, Earl slipped under the chain-link fence. Standing up on the neatly mowed lawn of the hospital, Earl felt like he just popped out of the rabbit hole. The woods and one giant, horny apeman separated from him by a fence; civilization and freedom lay straight ahead. Maybe not real freedom–he did just break into a mental hospital, but it was better than the domestic bliss Boner McMonkey offered. Earl began walking cautiously toward Ted.

"Oh, honey, you want to come with me? That is so

sweet! I wish I could take you both home, you beastly teddy bears."

A sorrowful howl rose from the other side of the fence. Earl turned to see Boner McMonkey puppy-dog eyed, reaching over the fence for Earl.

"O.M.G. This is exactly like *Casablanca!*" Ted squealed. Ted had no idea if it was like the movie; he'd never seen it. He just thought it sounded like something a homosexual would say.

Earl groaned, and hung his head. He then beckoned for Boner to follow. The creature shook his head. Avoiding people was deeply ingrained in all Bigfeet. Stepping into the human's world was insanity by Bigfoot standards. Earl shrugged and moved on. He'd offered. If the hairy hard-on didn't take him upon it, that was his problem.

The moaning grew louder, evolving into a wail punctuated with sobs. It sounded like a bloodhound was being passed through a truck engine.

If that thing doesn't shut up, I'm going to be busted, Earl thought to himself.

He beckoned for Bigfoot to follow him again as Ted informed him that both of them would need to stay in the woods.

"Shut up," Earl hissed at Ted.

Ted stared dumbstruck at Earl. The command had pulled Ted out of his role-playing. Now details were coming out; he was talking to a man in a Wookie costume.

"I don't know what you're doing, but that Bigfoot is my friend. I don't want to see anything happen to him. He needs to stay in the woods where he belongs." Ted felt like a parent explaining to a child why the toad found in the yard couldn't live in the house.

Earl whispered, "This is for his protection. Three

men are hunting him."

Ted absorbed the news. Suddenly, the path was clear. For a moment, Ted was able to push the medicated tablecloth off of his mental furniture. He always knew his time smoking with Bigfoot was incredible, and he realized how much he looked forward to seeing him. Their friendship was limited. Despite the interspecies differences, they were friends. Clarity sharpened Ted's mind, and he realized his time in the hospital was, in fact, him just hiding from his life. He wasn't getting better, because he liked the escape too much. A feeling welled up in Ted he hadn't felt in a long time: his life had purpose.

"We need to shut him up before the staff realizes it isn't an inmate howling," Ted said. Gone was the girly accent.

Earl watched as Ted shifted from flamer to Rusty Nail: Double Secret Operative for a government agency so secret, it had no name. It was only referred to in hushed tones as 'They.' As in, 'They said'. Ted's hip moved to a masculine position, the ascot was removed, the wrists straightened.

Earl stared dumbfounded at the metamorphoses. "Who the fuck are you?"

Ted / Rusty Nail fixed him with a confident stare, "I'm from the government. I'm here to help."

"Great."

Earl resumed beckoning to Boner, who only responded by howling louder.

"I've got an idea."

Earl turned seductively from Bigfoot, and smacked his ass. Immediately, the wailing stopped. Earl looked coyly over his shoulder at Boner, then wiggled his ass. He peeked again at Bigfoot, checking to see if he had his attention. Earl then went through all the moves he'd picked up from buying table dances at strip clubs. When he'd exhausted his moves, Bigfoot was dancing in place with an enormous grin plastered across his face.

Ted / Rusty Nail looked over at Earl, "I think you over did it."

Earl ignored the remark, and beckoned for Bigfoot. The giant stepped back several paces, then neatly hurdled the fence.

Earl looked at Ted / Rusty Nail as Boner jogged up. "You don't tell anyone about this, and I won't tell anyone about the . . . whatever you were doing before."

"Deal," Ted / Rusty Nail agreed.

Ted / Rusty Nail lead them to one end of a building, and told them to hide in the brush. "That door is a fire exit. You two hide here. I'll go check-in, then I'll open it from the inside."

38

"Lost Case of Being Found"
~Scott H. Biram

Ted, Earl and Boner were in Ted's room. The room was furnished with two single beds, each occupied by a Bigfoot or an impostor Bigfoot. Even sitting on the bed, Boner needed to hunch over to keep from breaking the acoustic ceiling tiles. His legs spread out from him nearly reached the other wall.

Ted/Rusty Nail was listening to the door, using a wax paper cup as an earpiece. Satisfied the hall was empty, Ted/Rusty Nail approached his two guests. He placed a comforting hand on Boner's shoulder. "I'm going to need to step out with your girlfriend for a minute. We'll be right back. Don't. Start. Howling. You need to be quiet." Bigfoot nodded.

As Earl and Ted/Rusty Nail moved toward the door, Bigfoot stood up. His head pushed up one of the ceiling tiles. Speaking towards the new hole in the ceiling, Ted assured Bigfoot it would be okay.

Ted listened to the door one more time. He then opened the door, and glanced around. The hall was clear. He beckoned for Earl to follow. In the hallway, Ted/Rusty Nail entered a vacant dorm room. Shutting the door behind them, Ted broke character again, "What the hell are you doing?"

Before answering, Earl pulled off the Chewbacca mask. He just stood there enjoying the fresh air on his face.

"Hello?" Ted waved his hand in front of Earl's

face. "Hey, I know you. You're the asshole with the paintball gun!"

Earl looked at Ted for the first time since removing the mask. He sighed, then launched into the entire story. He spoke rapidly; verbally ejaculating the story.

Ted raised his eyebrows when Earl finished the story. "And now what? What's the plan to get Bigfoot out of here?"

Earl shook his head, "I really don't know. I've just been reacting to these last twenty-four hours."

Stepping back into the Rusty Nail character, "Well, it's time to get proactive. I've never lost a man on my watch, and I'm not about to start."

The pep talk was interrupted by a loud thump from next door.

Earl and Ted/Rusty Nail dashed for the door. Ted/Rusty Nail stopped Earl from entering the hall. "Aren't you forgetting something?"

Earl grimaced at the thought of putting the mask back on. Feelings of claustrophobia enveloped him when he stuck his head back inside the mask's swampy atmosphere. "How do I look?"

"Great. Let's go."

Both men skidded to a halt inside Ted's room. Bigfoot sat on the floor, watching the contrails of his hand moving. He smiled contently as one of his eyes drifted lazily out of alignment.

Ted sighed, "He found my meds."

39

"Grown so Ugly"
~The Black Keys

Bigfoot feel great. Except think face may be melting. Not sure. Hands leaking color when Bigfoot move hand. Pretty cool, but not sure it good thing. Have to ask New She-Bigfoot how to put color back into Bigfoot.

Speaking of New She-Bigfoot, only outlaw for two days. Bigfoot in more trouble than ever been. Killed some Dark Agents. Now, Bigfoot staying in human den! Maybe being outlaw too exciting.

40

"Call When You're Ready"
~The Paybacks

Earl's Bluetooth chimed in his ear. He bumped his head to activate the device. "What?"

Sheriff Paan's voice answered, "Earl, we're on our way. You need to move Bigfoot to the hospital's cell block. It's on the first floor of building D. We'll meet you there."

"It may take some time. The horny ape got into a drug stash. He's fucking obliterated."

"Just get there."

Earl filled in Ted on the plan. Ted, who was no longer acting as secret agent, Rusty Nail, "I know where that is. We'll have to cross one of the break rooms to get there."

Something caught Earl's eye. "That thing always has a boner."

"He also took Viagra."

"You guys get dick-splints?"

"It's a long story. Should you be talking in front of him?"

"I don't think it matters at the moment. What did he take?"

"That's my winnings from the other patients. It would be easier to list the pills he didn't take."

Earl nodded, "How are we going to do this?"

"Well, I figured you'd use your feminine wiles on him again."

"Bullshit."

Slapping Earl's ass, "C'mon, get that labia mojo machine flapping."

Earl fixed a menacing stare at Ted, which was severely diluted by the Chewbacca mask, "Did I ever shoot you with a paintball?"

"Yeah, those things hurt."

"Good."

He bent down to Bigfoot–who'd gone kaleidoscope-eyes staring at the geometric patterns of the bed sheets—and tapped him on the shoulder. Bigfoot looked up, a lopsided grin formed at the sight of New She-Bigfoot. A paw clumsily grabbed for Earl, who easily dodged the grope. Earl walked to the door and beckoned Bigfoot to follow. Bigfoot drunkenly got to his feet. Ted and Earl were surprised he could stand, although he wobbled slowly. Like a video of a child playing hula hoop in slow-mo.

"Never underestimate what a man will do for his woman. Let's go," Ted said.

Ted could feel Earl stealing glances at him as they walked down the hallway. The ceilings in the hallways were taller than the rooms, so Bigfoot could walk without stooping, or attracting attention by breaking the ceiling tiles with his head.

"What?"

"What?" Earl responded.

"You're staring."

"It's just, you seem normal. What are you doing in here?"

Ted smiles, "I didn't deal with life outside very well."

"What exactly did you do?"

"The last time I was arrested? I was putting *Tested*

On Animals stickers on the condoms at Wal-Mart."

"They put you in here for that?"

"I was naked, and thought I was the Godiva Chocolate chick."

"Oh."

"It wasn't the first time."

Ted peered through the window in the break room's door. "We're going to have company. Just be cool."

Ted led the way into the break room as if everything was normal. The room was occupied by several patients in varying stages of lucidity. Don, Lyle, and Montgomery sat at a table in the corner playing Uno. Ted could tell by the collective look on their faces, he wasn't going to be able to breeze through without attracting attention. "Hi, guys."

Montgomery's normally stoic expression was replaced with sheer astonishment. Don dropped his cards, and slipped a hand underneath the table. To everyone's surprise, Lyle smiled, and raised his hand. Without missing a beat, Bigfoot gave him a high-five.

"What is going on, Ted?" Don asked, looking at the two apemen failing to look inconspicuous behind Ted.

"Uhm. Nothing. Why?" Ted asked innocently. He hoped he could convince them they were seeing things. He knew that plan was out when one of the other patients walked over and asked Earl if he was his mother.

"Okay, guys. Meet Bigfoot and his girlfriend. Government agents are after them. So I'm taking them to the old jail block so the sheriff can pick them up."

"We'll help," Lyle said, the second time any of them heard him speak.

One of the patients traded drooling for howling, fueled by the excitement in the room. Montgomery stood up, and stared down the howler, who wisely decided drooling was a safer activity.

Still staring at the howler, "Don, you are coming with us."

"Why?"

"Because Lyle said so!" Montgomery thundered.

41

"Redemption Song"
~Bob Marley

Earl opened the door, and he felt along the wall for the light switch. He felt the industrial aluminum cover screwed to the cinderblock wall. His fingers felt the switch and flicked it up. Cold, bright fluorescent light filled the cellblock.

Standing in the middle of the room were the three Dark Agents. They stood in a chevron formation, the tallest at the apex.

Bigfoot growled.

"Hello, Meh-Teh[39]. It is nice to see you again. As you can see, I have healed since our last meeting. You do know I can only be killed by one of my victims, don't you? My creator was reluctant to make me immortal. The caveat was my idea. I wished my method of mortality to be extremely difficult. You have already figured that out, didn't you? You stupid, fucking ape."

The entire tête-à-tête occurred in Bigfoot's language. Unable to comprehend the conversation, the humans were left to watch the growling ping pong between Bigfoot and the agent.

The howler from the break room wandered past the crowd. He was either ignoring the standoff, or simply oblivious. The group paused to watch him inspect the

---

[39] Meh-Teh, along with Yeti, are Himalayan words for the Abominable Snowman.

jail cells.

"Ah, Mr. Earl Stooge, I see you have returned to finish our conversation. If my memory is correct, I was about to shoot you. I wish you had not brought witnesses. I suppose it's a loser's nature. A blue crab will drag another escaping crab back down into the bucket. It makes it difficult on me. Do you have any idea how annoyed I'm going to get reloading this flintlock to kill each one of you?"

The howler drifted over, and poked the tallest Dark Agent as he spoke. The flintlock thundered. A crimson Rorschach splattered on the wall. If tested, more than one person in the room would have stated the ink blot looked a lot like a giant footprint. Howler twisted, giving the group a clear look at the silver dollar sized tunnel through his skull. He fell backwards on to the cement floor. His skull make an out-of-tune bongo thump. "You see? I have not killed you yet, and I already have to reload."

The door on the opposite side of the room opened. Sunlight spilled in through the opening, silhouetting six people stepping in to the room. The other two agents spun, and drew their weapons.

Sheriff Paan and Deputy O'Boogie drew their weapons in response. "Tioga County Sheriff. Lay down your weapons, and place your hands on your head." Sheriff Paan commanded. Harry and Jeff fanned out from behind the peacekeepers. Each leveled a dart gun at a Dark Agent.

Earl realized his group was the backstop if the shooting started. He nudged Ted, then guided Bigfoot out of the line of fire. The rest of the herd split. Moses parting the seas, brought to you by Colt and Glock firearms.

The tallest Dark Agent sneered at his unloaded

flintlock. He replaced the antique into the left shoulder holster. He drew a Desert Eagle .50 handgun from his right side. The movement was quick. It was drawn by the time Sheriff Paan's brain realized what just happened. The pistol hung loosely in the agent's hand, pointing at the floor.

The observers gawked at the pistol. It wasn't a gun, it was a howitzer without wheels. The weapon often makes cameos in Arnold Schwarzenegger movies. It is one of the few handguns which looks normal in his massive hands.

Sheriff Paan repeated his commands. None of the Dark Agents moved.

The door behind the Sheriff opened. Echo and Roger the cameraman walked in to the middle of the standoff. "I guess this is where the party is."

Echo waved at the two Dark Agents. Both agents visibly recoiled at the memory of the bear spray. "Sheriff, those are the two men who broke into my apartment."

"Darlin', I'm trying to arrest them. They aren't taking it too well."

Echo nodded towards the jail cells a few feet from the Dark Agents, "At least you won't have to take them far."

Assuming command of the situation, the tallest Dark Agent ordered, "You and your men stand down, Sheriff. You are out of your pay grade."

"Not happening, hound dog. You and your men lay down your weapons. Get into those cells, and we'll sort this whole thing out."

"We are federal agents, Sheriff. I am taking these two creatures into custody."

"What do you want with them?" Sheriff Paan

asked. He was trying to buy time. *Do these guys know one of those things is a guy in a monkey suit?*

"Okay, Sheriff. By the way, I have been wanting to let you in on a little secret. I was in the Oval Office when your idol visited. I was consulting Mr. Nixon on our analysis of the effects of LSD we leaked to the public. Your idol pulled the .45 out of his ridiculous jumper. The Secret Service agents were caught completely off guard. I, however, was not. I dropped that hip-shaking clown where he stood."

"I remember," Sheriff Paan said. "You and your men stand down."

"Not your decision. You should have concentrated on your karaoke career," The tallest Dark Agent said as he pointed his gun at Bigfoot.

"No!" Lyle bellowed, jumping in front of Bigfoot: The Catatonic Priest of Human Shields. The shot grazed Lyle's head. The hit wasn't fatal, but his hair would never part the same.

Montgomery launched himself at the agents, catching the tallest Dark Agent off guard. The tallest agent stumbled into Bigfoot, who grabbed his throat. Montgomery grabbed the left agent, who was lining Deputy O'Boogie in his sights. Montgomery moved in front of the agent, using his momentum to spin the smaller man into the wall. It was a medium he wasn't used to, but a definite snow angel impression was made in the cinderblocks.

Earl tackled the second agent as Ted wrestled the gun from his hand. Montgomery joined the pig pile.

Neither Sheriff Paan or Deputy O'Boogie could get a clear shot. Both men advanced to join the melee. Harry had a clear shot of the agent who bounced off the wall. He slowly squeezed the trigger. The tranquilizer dart hit the agent in the thigh.

The tallest Dark Agent's throat strained against the hairy paw squeezing it. "I told you, you stupid ape: I can only be killed by one of my victims." He pressed the barrel against Bigfoot's forehead.

Elvis's pistol thundered. The tallest agent's head slammed to the side. A small diameter hole trickled blood on the entry side; an opening the diameter of a coffee mug on the opposite side. A funnel through the brain pan. Bullet the Blue Sky[40]. The agent's head turned, and looked at Sheriff Flan Paan. "You can't be . . ." The agent dissolved in Bigfoot's hand. Streams of dust fell from the empty suit as it fluttered to the ground.

The other two agents also dissolved into powder.

Echo stepped up to the sheriff. She placed her hand on his; guiding the gun down. "So, you really are Elvis reincarnated?"

Sheriff Paan flashed that famous smile, "'You got your show, and I got mine[41].'"

<42>

---

[40] "Bullet the Blue Sky", written by Bono and U2.
[41] What Elvis Presley said to President Nixon during the 1970 meeting in the Oval Office when Nixon commented on Elvis's outfit.

Epilogue

Lyle's head healed. The gunshot left him deaf in his left ear, but he never had another catatonic episode. No longer displaying any symptoms, he was released from the hospital. Lyle successfully lobbied for Montgomery's release, provided that he remain under Lyle's supervision. They now own a themed art gallery downtown. The theme? Customers pay to have snow angel impressions of their bodies on canvas. A cross between paint-your-own-pottery and midget tossing. The gallery is hugely popular with the S&M crowd.

Don remains a resident of the hospital. He is no longer prescribed Viagra. Self-restraint is a new focal point of his treatment.

Ian King's skeleton was discovered by hunters the next fall. There are no suspects in his murder.

Ted was also released from the asylum. He moved to California where he can make a living with his doppelganger personality: he became an actor.

Sheriff Flan Paan and Deputy Winston O'Boogie both resigned from law enforcement. Sheriff Paan decided the world still needed Elvis. He's recording an album of original material. Winston O'Boogie is his manager.

Earl Stooge ran for sheriff of Tioga County, New York. His campaign slogan was 'It takes a criminal to catch a criminal.' He won by a landslide.
Patch became Earl's deputy. The accurate

inventory of the evidence room is still questionable.

Echo Clyne received national attention for her expose on government conspiracies. She was promoted to station manager. Roger is still her cameraman. There was no mention of Bigfoot in her newscast.

Southern Tier Bigfoot Tours is still open for business; under new management. Jeff and Roy made the national news when they provided DNA and biopsied tissue samples of Bigfoot. The validity of the samples are still being analyzed. Roy created an i-Phone application that converts Bigfoot's language to human speech.

The new sheriff successfully persuaded the State of New York to grant a large track of forest for 'some bullshit scientific purpose'. Trespassing is strictly prohibited. Several nights a week a party can be heard deep in the woods. Elvis is the only music ever played.

Harry wrote a book: *A Hoaxer's Guide to Hoaxing Bigfoot*. It was not a bestseller. Domino forgave Harry after learning he hadn't lied. She then dumped him when she found out he had shot paintballs at her patients. She took him back when he finished writing his book. Harry came to his senses and proposed to Domino. She no longer speaks in lyrics.
Her girlfriends still know he's the stupidest man in the world.

Bigfoot returned to the woods where he makes occasional appearances for the Bigfoot tours. In exchange for not raiding campers of their gear, he is supplied with cigarettes and whiskey. He was also given a lighter he can use and a steady supply of peanut butter and banana sandwiches.

Bigfoot eventually got over losing New She-Bigfoot.

43

Excerpt from *A Hoaxer's Guide to Hoaxing Bigfoot*

The thing with planting evidence–I call it 'seeding'–the thing with seeding is the quality of the specimen left, and the likelihood of someone finding it. You wouldn't believe how many samples I've left that have been ignored by every hiker and bird-watcher in the county. I've left a wool sweater of Bigfoot hair without one person giving it a second look. I swear with some people, Bigfoot would have to be on fire and running directly at them before they noticed.

Hair is hard to plant as evidence; harder than you'd think. For one, getting quality hair is difficult. Human hair usually has a distinctive cut edge which totally gives it away when viewed under a microscope. It's difficult to find any human hair which has not been cut. Don't even think about a baby's hair. Baby hair is fine and soft; no one would believe Bigfoot would be covered in it.

You have to assume the hair you plant, if found, will face serious consideration under the microscope. Tricinologists, those folks who precisely identify hair samples, aren't going to be fooled by a totally bogus sample. Scale patterns and pigmentation can't match any local indigenous animals. Ideally, the hair you leave will lack a continuous medullary core. The absence of a medullary core will suggest a primate, but isn't specific enough of a note to narrow down what type. You also want to try to acquire hair in the telogen stage of hair growth cycle. The telogen stage means the hair was ready to be naturally shed. Also, don't try to mix human and animal hair to fool the lab. The hair strands are tested individually. They aren't boiled down in a soup pot. Besides, the scaling and pigmentation will never match.

Your success as a Bigfoot hoaxer also depends on the lab where the hair is sent. The tricinologist is going to compare your seed hair against a known database of hairs. If you are lucky, the hair is only compared with regional candidates. A hair sample found in the northeastern United States may not be compared with an orangutan's hair sample. If you are lucky, your sample will go up against a moose, elk, badger, skunk, coyote, bear, etc- an animal expected to be cruising around the North American woods. In that case, the hair is moved to what is called an indeterminate category. You see, a sample has to be measured against something known- like human hair is measured against a database of human hair. But, if the lab can't identify what type of hair it is- your sample goes into the 'I don't know what the fuck it is' category. This is the money shot of seeding: your sample could not be categorically dismissed as a hoax, and it could not be identified with any known animal. Your sample is now is as mysterious as the creature it allegedly came from. I call this the Cryptozoological Catch 22. The evidence can't be dismissed, but it also doesn't prove anything except it is hair. I can sell tours for years based on one sample lucky enough to fall in this category.

Bigfoot hunters love to point out the hair sample couldn't be identified in a lab. They think it adds credibility to their work. They'll point out this sort of evidence to anyone who will listen. Evidence like this will be referenced in websites, in books, at conferences.

This is the holy sacrament of true believers. Like I said: having hair analyzed in a lab is about as useful as the Pope's balls as far as positively identifying Bigfoot. There is no known Bigfoot hair to compare it against. There isn't a master sample to use as a control group. This is the same argument against obtaining DNA from a hair- without known Bigfoot DNA; you've got nothing but unidentified DNA.

You may wonder why the lab doesn't keep testing the sample until a match is found. Simple answer: funding and time. Labs don't make money wasting capital on figuring out every specimen. After testing, your sample will be assigned an inventory number and will be stored in a climate-controlled warehouse somewhere. By the way, it's also a win-win for the lab. The lab still collects a full fee for analyzing evidence it couldn't come up with a conclusive determination of.

You see, first you try to get some interest in an area by faking a sighting or footprints. Then you seed the area with some evidence. Not immediately and not in the exact same area. You have to wait until the investigators pack their bags, but before public interest goes away. In a small town like this, this is the biggest thing to happen to this town since Sarah Macalister posed for Playboy Magazine back in the '70s . . .

Acknowledgements

I would like to thank the following:

My dad and Honu, for your endless support and advice. Even if I didn't deserve the first, and ignored the second. Jonah and Finn, for helping to remember to use my imagination. Julie Monaco, for one great suggestion. Mike Baird, for being enough of a neanderthal to serve as a model for Bigfoot. Stanley Francis and Shawna Szabo, for all of your support. Kristin "Saint" St. Mary and Michael Flanigan for looking out for me. Jared Klossner for building the website. To all of the writers who helped me along the way (Phil Polizatto, Lance Carbuncle, Marcus Edder, and Robert Tacoma).

Also, to all of the Bigfoot researchers and hoaxers, for giving me something to write about.

Author's Bio:

Noah Baird wanted to attend the Ringling Bros. and Barnum & Bailey Clown College, but his grades weren't good enough (who knew?). However, his grades were good enough to fly for the U.S. Navy (again, who knew?), where he spent 14 years until the government figured out liberal, vegetarian, surfers don't make the best military aviators. He has also worked as a stand-up comedian in Hawaii for Japanese tourists, where the language barrier really screwed up some great jokes. On the bright side, a sailboat was named after the punchline of one of his jokes.

He has several political satire pieces published on The Spoof under the pen name orioncrew. Noah received his bachelors in Historical and Political Sciences from Chaminade University, where he graduated magna cum laude. He knows nothing about hoaxing Bigfoot. This is his first novel.

CPSIA information can be obtained at www.ICGtesting.com
Printed in the USA
BVOW080956031011

272697BV00009B/47/P